WHEN LOVES HITS LIKE
CHRISTMAS

MICHELLE MITCHELL

ACKNOWLEDGMENTS

Thank you, Lord, for yet another opportunity to share this gift with the world. I feel blessed to be able to do something I love and I pray I can do this forever.

To Author Rhonda McKnight and Author Sherri Lewis, thank you for reviewing my work and pushing me to see this project through. The dream team strikes again!

I want to say thank you to my beta readers, Author Sherron Elise, who is one of my favorite authors. If you haven't checked out her work yet, please go one-click one of her titles today.

Thank you to Covers in Color for another amazing wrap. And a huge thank you to everyone who has stayed on me about getting this project completed! I appreciate your energy in wanting to read this story and your encouragement for me to keep at it.

To all of the readers, book clubs, and podcast who have supported me from day one and for those who are getting their first introduction to me this year, I appreciate you and hope you'll enjoy this labor of love.

ALSO BY MICHELLE MITCHELL

ONE

Christmas Eve, 2018

My coworker, Joelle, handed the customer her tickets and cut her eyes in my direction. I let out a low chuckle and shook my head because I knew she would have a lot to say about this lady. The woman hadn't even made it across the room before I heard Joelle mumble, "Ol', heifer."

"I beg your pardon," the woman said, turning on her heels.

"Oh, she wished you a Merry Christmas," I said, in an attempt to diffuse the situation. We had several travelers waiting to board their flight, and the last thing either of us needed was for one of them to complain about the customer service.

The woman's eyes narrowed but she left without incident. I shook my head and swatted Joelle's arm as she tapped into the computer. She dabbed at her forehead with the back of her hand as her mahogany complexion glistened under the bright lights.

"Whew, chile. It's toasty in here. Can you call maintenance? Did they turn the heat on?" Joelle complained as she swept her braids into a ponytail.

I gave her a sideways glance. "Maybe if you'd stop acting up with these customers, you wouldn't be feeling like damnation's child. You gotta ease up, sis."

"Audie, if you think I'm going to hell, you could just say that you know." She shrugged. "And anyway, you know good and durn well I didn't tell that gremlin to have a merry anything. She comes in here all miserable and thinks we have to take it. Tuh, she got the right one today."

I started to respond but snapped my mouth shut, deciding it was best to leave it alone. Joelle was seven months pregnant and I could already tell today wasn't going to be a good day. She was cranky and our shift had just started. We were Gate Agents with Southern Skies airline. I'd started working for the company three years ago, and Joelle was going on her fifth year.

Her burn out was evident. Joelle's patience with customers was nonexistent. Before pregnancy gave her a valid reason to miss work, Joelle always found a reason to leave early or call out sick, and then she managed to find a way to get out of helping customers. And she was the queen of extended lunches. But she wasn't all bad though. At least sixty percent of the time, she didn't pop off at the customers.

"Look, I'll check on the air for you, but only because I want to make sure my goddaughter is okay."

She chuckled as her hand freely rubbed her swollen stomach. "Thank you. You need to tell her to sit down and give her mommy a break. She's kicking my behind today."

I smiled. "See, even lil' mama is out here trying to get you to behave. Anyway, what's going on for Christmas at the Reed house this weekend?"

"Samuel is frying a turkey, and the in-laws are driving in from Alabama. They are going to make all of the sides and have insisted I not lift a finger. Trust and believe, I'm taking them up on the offer. The only finger I'll be lifting is the one holding a fork," Joelle said with a wink.

I chuckled and pulled my hair up into a chignon. Joelle was right. It had started to get warm in here. "Well good. You need to take advantage of every opportunity you get to stay off of your feet. Maybe it will assist with your stank attitude."

"I'm afraid to ask what your plans are, but I tell you what if they include Rodney ol' dried up behind, just spare me the details." Joelle shook her head in disgust as her lips turned up so far it looked like she had tried to smell them.

I shooed her away. "Whatever. We're going to cook dinner together tonight, open our gifts by candlelight, and then join my parents at their house on Christmas Day."

Joelle's eyes shifted back and forth, and I could see the wheels spinning. I inhaled deeply, not wanting to hear what Rodney hate she was going to spew next. "Have you met his parents? Every Christmas, you say y'all are going to your folk's place, but never his people. Don't they live in Georgia too?"

"Yes, of course, I've met them, and yes, they live here." I shrugged. "He says they don't celebrate Christmas the way my family does. Like, they don't have family over or cook a big meal. They just exchange cash and call it a day."

"Is that what they told you, or did Rodney feed you that lie?"

I sighed. "Stop it. Why would he need to lie? It's what he shared with me when we first started dating."

She pursed her lips. "Interesting. Five years and you have never spent the holidays with his family. I'm perplexed. Now tell me this, how many times have you hung out with them?"

"I don't know. Once or twice at family barbecues. I don't like what you're implying. I'm not a hidden girlfriend." I diverted my eyes to the woman approaching. I was glad for the reprieve because conversations about Rodney always led to Joelle interrogating me about my relationship and asking when I was going to call it quits.

The elderly woman hobbled to the counter like her shoes were trying to go in the opposite direction. Her curly wig had a gangster lean. I wanted to shift it a little, but I didn't know if she'd curse me out for trying to help. She smiled at me and said, "Excuse me. Can I—"

"One second, don't you hear us trying to have a conversation?" Joelle scolded the woman. "If you'll have a seat, I'll call you back over in a few minutes."

"Ma'am, don't mind her. It's the hormones," I said, pointing towards Joelle's bump. I reached out to grab the woman's boarding pass. "Here, I can help you."

The woman glowered at Joelle and turned to me with a grateful smile. My work mother, as I lovingly called Joelle, could care less about the woman giving her the stink eye as she clicked her tongue against the back of her teeth and proceeded to interrogate me.

"Okay, let me make sure I have this math right cause something ain't adding up. Five years as a couple. Only met his parents once. Broke up and got back together again twice. And after all this… no ring… girl, if you don't stop leasing out that car and look for someone ready to drive it full-time, I know something."

The woman tittered at Joelle's comment, covering her mouth with her free hand as she reached up to take her ticket. As the woman headed back to her seat, I rolled my eyes and mumbled, "I know she didn't just laugh in my face. Ol' heifer."

"Uh-huh," Joelle said. "See there, you should've made her wait. She sniggling all in your face."

"Sniggling?" My brows rose and I shook my head. "I don't think you're using the right word."

"She was snickering and giggling… that's sniggling. Don't correct me. Either way, she was doing it at your expense."

"Oh hush," I said, unable to hold back a laugh as I saw Joelle's mouth twitch. "But to answer your question, I've spoken with them on the phone a few times. Or well, I've spoken to his mom, not so much his dad."

"Uh-huh, and what y'all talk about?"

I stammered. "Um, shoot... I don't know just... um, whatever's going on at the time. But you can just chill. It's not a big deal, so you can park those thoughts in your head. As long as Rodney and I are communicating, the rest will fall into place."

She looked at me quizzically before turning away. "Yeah, okay. Oh, and speaking of things coming together... your favorite customer, the one you need to be giving some attention, is headed this way."

"Huh?" I turned my head from side to side until my eyes landed on him. Business-class Bae. Or Davon Hampton, as listed on his boarding pass. His job required him to travel a lot and I was fortunate enough to check him in on several occasions. He was kind, funny, and unlike me—he was available. Wasn't that always the case? When you're single, there's hardly anyone trying to holler at you. But the minute you get involved with someone, the number of men waiting on your phone number is longer than the line of men waiting on the new Jordan sneakers to drop. Our conversations were innocent enough and started over my desire to have a white Christmas.

"Headed back to Colorado, huh? Is this trip for business or pleasure, Mr. Hampton?"

"You've checked my boarding pass at this gate at least twenty times, and you still won't call me, Davon," he said, as he shook his head. "Mr. Hampton is my dad. And yes, I'll be headed to Denver and it's for business and pleasure. You know I have to visit my family when I go back home."

I mused. "I've never been, but I hear it's beautiful. Guess you'll be having a white Christmas. I'm jealous. I'm sure it's not a big deal to you since you grew up in a state that gets snow. You'd have to live in the Georgia mountains to get a real chance of a snowflake sighting. This time last year, I could've put on shorts to go outside if I wanted. It's ridiculous." I returned his pass and smiled. "Well, enjoy your flight, Davon."

He drummed his fingers on the counter and smirked. "You know what?"

My brows lifted. "Nope. What is it?"

His head dropped and he shook his head again. "Never mind. Let me stop."

"Wait, what were you going to say?" I asked before he could walk away.

He pressed his lips together, which caused his dimples to pop out before he spoke again. "I don't know. I just… something inside of me says I'm going to be the one to take that trip with you one day."

I frowned. "Huh? What trip?"

"To Colorado," he said with a shrug. "Or anywhere you want to go to have a white Christmas. I'd love to be able to share the moment with you."

My eyes bugged and I chuckled. "You don't even know me, and I don't think my boyfriend would like this little trip you have planned for us."

"Trust me, I've been trying to learn you at a distance." He shrugged and smiled. "I know it may sound ridiculous, but I think we met for a reason. I've been to this airport several times and I've met lots of people, but I feel like there is good energy between us. Is it just me?"

It wasn't just him, but I never told him so. I never admitted to feeling the connection he was referencing because that would make it real and I was in a relationship. That was two years ago, back when I was in year three with Rodney and thinking he'd finally propose. Now here I was in my fifth year with no ring and no engagement insight. Davon was the fantasy. He was great on paper, but there was no guarantee he wasn't just a Rodney remix, waiting to be discovered. It wasn't worth the risk.

"Look at you… he's got you in a trance," Joelle said with a smirk.

I giggled. "He is fine."

"Mmmhmm, handsome, tall, such a gentleman, and a beautiful deep, dark coffee brown." She nudged me. "So, you gonna bite that shiny apple today, Eve?"

I rolled my eyes. "No forbidden fruit for me. Davon has made it clear he's interested in me and I've always resisted. Today isn't going to be any different. You know I'm—"

"With Rodney's trifling behind?" Joelle interjected and waved me away. "Girl, bye. Dumping him needs to be your New Year's resolution. Matter of fact, make that a gift to yourself. I'm so tired of hearing about him. You need to unwrap something new this Christmas."

"Hush before he hears you," I hissed as my eyes shot in his direction. "You know you don't know how to whisper. And anyway, even when things got shaky, I never cheated or had a desire to cheat. Rodney and I have issues, but what relationship is perfect? We're good. It's fine."

Joelle's lips twisted as she nodded. "Uh-huh, tell that to the saliva coming out of your mouth."

My hand flew to my mouth and Joelle erupted in laughter. I knew she was joking, but I still dabbed at my lips. "Shut up. You play too much."

My eye slipped back to Davon. Why did he have to be so handsome? Scratch that—he should come with a warning label because the man was break-your-neck-going-in-for-second-looks sexy.

"If it isn't my two favorite Southern Skies agents. How you ladies doing?" he said, breaking into my thoughts.

I leaned over the counter and grinned at him. His subtle, woodsy cologne surrounded me like a warm embrace. Not only was he attractive, but he smelled so yummy. "Hey, Davon. Welcome back. I see you're heading home."

"Yep. Back to Denver. I'll be settling in there for at least a year. We have a new client and I'm getting them set up and hosting training sessions on the new software my company launched."

"A year? Well, I hope you packed with some sense. Remember last time, you came back telling us that hawk almost cut you in half. I've never been to Denver, but even I know if you go this time of year, you'll need a coat with some type of lining," Joelle said.

He chuckled. "Hey, it had been a minute since I'd been back home. This Georgia weather got me spoiled. But yes, mom, I brought a heavier coat this time around. To be honest, I'd be happier if I had someone to join me in my travels. A coat is nice, but I'd much rather be wrapped up with my love and a warm blanket."

My face flushed as the sizzle of his stare warmed my skin. I didn't know what it was about him, but whenever he was close, my heart pounded through my chest as if someone was using it as a punching bag. I allowed my eyes to connect with his and instantly regretted it. His magnetic smile and intoxicating cologne begged me to say forget Rodney and hop on the plane to join him in Colorado.

"Mmhmm, I agree, Davon. Stop me if I'm wrong, but I think you're seeking someone who has a radiant smile, golden complexion, long auburn hair, and soft brown eyes," Joelle chimed in. "Come to think of it, that sounds like Audrienne. If only we could convince her to get rid of her loser boyfriend. Then you'd have everything you need, huh?"

I glared at her. "Seriously, Joelle, he didn't say anything about me traveling with him. He only said he needed to find someone."

"Well, actually, in one of our early conversations, I told you I wanted to share a White Christmas with you. The offer is still open." He licked his lips and tilted his head to the side as he looked at me. "So yeah, you could be... no you are the one I'm speaking of—I'm just waiting on you, Audie."

I smiled and turned my attention to the screen. "It's like I keep telling you though, I have a boyfriend."

"But you could have a whole man, honey," Joelle said as she folded her arms across her chest. "A man who got some real plans he wants to put in place. I like that, Davon."

I swallowed hard. My body was in sensory overload. My mouth felt dry and my body tingled from head to toe. I needed to shake this feeling and redirect the conversation. "Anyway, I'm surprised to see you here so early. You've got a few hours until your flight departs."

His shoulders slumped as he shoved his hands into the front pockets of his khakis. "Yeah. I just thought I'd get settled in and maybe grab something to eat. And, I kind of hoped I could use some of the time stealing moments with my favorite Southern Skies employee."

"You are too much, Davon. What are you thinking about eating?" I asked, trying to change the subject. "With this airport being your second home, I'm sure you've probably tried everything in here."

Joelle chortled. "From the looks of it, what he wants ain't on nobody's menu."

I glared at her. "Joelle, stop messing with this man."

"She's right, Audie. I was hoping you'd let me take you to lunch. And before you say it, I know you're in a relationship. But you've got to eat at some point today, right? No harm in us doing it at the same time and in the same place." He bit down on his bottom lip and leaned toward me. "So, what do you think?"

My hands formed a praying position in front of my face because God was gonna have to help me with this one. Every inch of my body said yes – heck it was screaming *hell* yes –

but I wasn't about to put myself in a situation-ship with Davon. What if the chemistry between us was real?

Several scenarios ran through my head on where one lunch with him would lead, and then I reasoned the validity in Davon's statement—I did need to eat. And anyway, it wasn't like I was pursuing anything. This was about grabbing food and having a little small talk in between bites. I ate with my male coworkers all of the time. This was not as huge a deal as I was making it out to be. So, it was settled. I'd accept his invitation.

"She's interested," Joelle interjected before I could respond. "Her break is in an hour, and you can take her anywhere because she's not a picky eater."

He looked to me for confirmation, and the corners of his mouth rose as I nodded. "Perfect. It's a date."

Davon turned and started in the opposite direction. As I watched him, his words finally registered with me. "It's not a date," I called after him. He looked over his shoulder at me and winked before he disappeared into the sea of people roaming the airport. I turned to Joelle and scowled. "Why'd you do that? I can speak for myself."

She shrugged. "You were taking too long to answer and you know good and darn well you want a sample of that man. Don't you?"

I pressed my lips together and tried not to laugh. She was right, but I wasn't gonna tell her what I was feeling. Heck, I wasn't sure what I was feeling. Instead, I rolled my eyes and got back to work. I laughed under my breath. Who was I fooling? I couldn't concentrate on anything with Davon taking up residence in my mind. I knew it was wrong, but I was anxious to see him. This was not a date. It was just lunch. But why was I so excited to see him again?

TWO

An hour later, we walked into one of the newer additions to the airport, Flavor 101. I hadn't had a chance to eat here yet but was excited to try something new with someone new. As we neared the table, I was shocked to see he'd taken it upon himself to put a few candles down to create ambience and there was a single rose laying across my place setting.

"Davon, wow. This is so sweet, but a bit too romantic, don't you think?" I asked, sitting as he pulled out a chair for me.

He lowered into the seat across from me and frowned. "Actually, all of the tables have candles on them but they aren't lit. As for the rose, I'm not sure how we got too lucky to snag the only table with one, but I'm sorry, I can't take any credit for this."

My eyes scanned the room and my mouth dropped. I was so embarrassed. "My bad. I shouldn't have assumed any— wait, are you playing with me?"

Davon busted out laughing and I sighed with relief. "I'm sorry, Audrienne. I couldn't resist messing with you."

"Dang, okay." I leaned back in my chair and smirked. "Who knew you'd be a prankster?"

He threw up his hands. "The restaurant had the candles, but I was able to grab the rose from one of the vendors. I figured one, red rose wouldn't be coming on too strong, but I guess I was wrong."

"It's cool and I'll accept this gift, but don't make a habit of it."

He chuckled. "My bad. I'll try my best to resist the urge to express myself in ways that could be deemed to be romantic. But I have to admit, you telling me not to make it a habit makes me feel like you're giving me the green light to surprise you on occasion."

I wagged my finger at him and grinned. "Very clever. I appreciate your attempt to work in a loophole, but you know that's not what I meant."

His brow raised and a slow smile spread across his face. I inhaled deeply. I had a feeling my verbal no didn't match the flirtatious glint in my eyes.

"I like what you did to your hair. It looks nice," he said.

I raised a hand to my hair which I hadn't secured with any bobby pins when I pulled it into a bun earlier. From the feel of it, I had loose strands hanging about and the chignon was crooked and felt more like a chig-not. I scrunched my nose up. "Really? It's a tad on the messy side. Joelle hates when I wear my hair in a bun."

He shook his head and smiled. "No, I meant the color. You got highlights – gold or maybe blonde—it looks good on you."

"Oh, yeah. It's a few months old now. Thanks for noticing."

My cheeks warmed and I diverted my eyes away from him. I grabbed the menu to find a less problematic activity to indulge in besides staring into his deep brown eyes. This was why I tried to avoid an intimate setting with him. The heat between us was evident and a large part of me didn't want it to cool down.

"Uh, I guess we better go ahead and order before my break is over."

His dimple acknowledged my attempt to break the obvious tension between us and he reached to take the menu away from me. "I hope you don't mind. Since Joelle said you weren't a picky eater, I went ahead and ordered us a few things to try off the appetizer menu since I know we don't have much time. I wanted them to bring it out shortly after we sat."

"Oh, okay. I guess that was a good idea. It'll give me a chance to check out your palate."

"Was that a douche move? It was, wasn't it? Dang. Sorry. I was so excited you agreed to join me, I guess I jumped the gun." He passed the menu back to me. "I went about this all wrong. Here, look to see what you might want to eat. If you want, you can take some of what I ordered home for dinner, or have it if you get hungry later."

Without thinking, I reached across the table and put my hand on top of his. "It's okay. Really... the appetizers I saw on the menu all looked very tempting. I'm sure it'll be fine."

He looked down at my hand and his shoulders relaxed. His eyes raised to mine and once again, I was stuck in the allure of his gaze. I couldn't explain it but I felt seen in his eyes. There was a longing behind his gaze and I wanted to stay lost there because I felt it too. We hardly knew one another, but this pull between us was nonsensical. It was emotional I supposed.

It amazed me how two people could feed off of each other's energy and have a desire to build a connection with each other. Perhaps I'd been in my current relationship too long and had forgotten what this felt like. But one thing was for sure... I wasn't ready to let go of this feeling.

"Do you remember the first time we had lunch together?" he asked, his mouth curved into a smile.

I noticed my hand was still touching his and slide it away

as I laughed. "If memory serves me correctly, you hijacked my lunch. There was plenty of people sitting alone, but you came to my table saying there was nowhere to sit."

His head bobbed. "Maybe so, but you didn't tell me no. Sounds like you didn't mind my company."

My lips twisted and I shook my head as I fought back a smile. I thought about that day often. The first time I met Davon officially, was in the food court at the airport. My break was just about over when he approached my table and asked to sit with me.

"Mind if I sit down?" a male voice said. "There's no place else to sit."

I looked up to see a handsome, familiar face and smirked. "Sure. Except for the table over there with the elderly man. Then there's the one —"

He sat his things down on the table and held up his hand. "Okay. You got me. There are a few other single-occupant tables, but there was only one that included you."

"Mmhmm." I took a sip of my drink and smiled. "So, remind me of your name again? I recall your face but we get so many travelers that I don't always know the names. I'm Audrienne Wilson by the way."

"Davon Hampton," he said. He leaned back in his chair and took a sip of his coffee. A smile danced on his lips as she pulled the cup away to speak. "I guess it's good you at least remember my face. I certainly can't forget yours."

My mouth parted to speak, but I was rendered speechless. "Uh. Wow. Aren't you a flirt? I appreciate the compliment but I have a boyfriend."

"He's fortunate. I'm sure he's thanking God on the regular for blessing him with such an amazing woman."

I shook my head. "Amazing? You don't even know me."

He put his elbows on the table and leaned in closer. "I've passed through this airport a multitude of times, and have spoken with you enough times to see your heart. Every time you smile it shines through and anyone with eyes should be able to see it."

That was the start of everything. Whenever he traveled, whether he was boarding at my gate or not, he made it his business to stop by and see me. With each meeting, my walls came down and I started to look forward to the chance to get a moment of his time. It was a dangerous game, but I didn't want to give it up. I felt like as long as I didn't allow things to get too personal, I wasn't breaking any rules. This lunch, however, made me feel like the lines were about to get blurred.

"Okay. We can't just sit here and not talk," he said, breaking my thoughts and bringing me back to the present. "I need to learn more about my future wife. I mean friend." I cocked my head to the side and he chuckled. "So, tell me everything. What makes you happy? I'm trying to get to know you, so don't hold back."

"Get to know me as a friend? Or… are you…I mean, are you wanting—"

"More? Yes, if the timing was right, but I'm respecting your relationship." A mischievous grin touched the corners of his mouth. "Back to my question, what brings you joy?"

I pressed my tongue to the inside of my cheek as I tried to hold back a smile. "Okay. Well, I like to sing, though I probably sound like a raccoon stuck in a trap. I also enjoy cooking and wine tastings."

"Oh snap. What's your specialty?" he asked.

My shoulders lifted as I blushed. "I can do a little of everything. I love soul food, but I can throw down on some seafood dishes too."

"That's what's up." His head bobbed and he leaned into the table and said, "What else? I know last Christmas when I was headed home, you mentioned you planned to spend time with your family too."

"Yeah. We get together at my parent's house every

Christmas to open gifts and eat. My family is very important to me. We are very close. My mom is my best friend. I tell her everything. She is my strength."

"Same. Family is key. I talk to my parents several times a week on the phone and video chats. I have a lot of relatives but I'm an only child. My cousins are my brothers and sisters. I don't know where'd I be without any of them. What about you?"

I smirked. "I have a little, big brother. He's so overprotective of me. He can't stand my boyfriend. He doesn't think he's good enough for me. But what's funny about that is my brother is a womanizer. We can't keep his women straight at the family functions. Even still, my brother has had my heart since the day he was born."

"So, speaking of your boyfriend, how's it going with him?"

I shrugged. "As good as can be expected, you know? All couples have good and bad days."

The waiter came over with an assortment of dishes. The steam rose from a plate of lemon pepper wings which included celery and both ranch and bleu cheese dressing. My stomach started to growl as I eyed the platter holding the Thai, chili shrimp tacos with cilantro slaw, veggie spring rolls, and baked zucchini fries.

"Can I get you anything else?" The waiter asked.

Davon looked at me and I shook my head no. Everything looked so good.

"Would you mind bringing us a few to-go boxes and the ticket? I want to take care of those things now since we have a time constraint," Davon said to the waiter as he started away from the table.

"You did well. This all looks great," I said, as I piled my plate with a spring roll, fries, and a few wings.

He slipped me a curious glance before putting a few items on his dish. "Can I ask you another question, Audie?"

I took a bite of the spring roll and chewed slowly. I considered how he'd just asked about my relationship and felt a bit guarded. I hoped he wasn't going to ask anything else about me and Rodney. "I'm not certain I finished answering the first question, but sure, what is it?"

"What's the percentage of the good and the bad?"

My eyes widened. When he said he had a question, I didn't anticipate it being this loaded. "Whoa. Umm, you went there. Well, uh… Rodney and I have gone through so much together. Regardless of how hard it gets, we still battle through and I think that means something, don't you?"

As the words left my mouth, even I felt like I was in a crappy situation. Rodney and I only communicated to argue and intimacy was nonexistent. I was pretty sure he was hooking up with someone other than me and what made this sadder was I didn't care. And if I was honest, I was only still there because I couldn't make myself walk away. I'd invested too much time into this relationship. I couldn't just give all of that up, could I?

"How long has it been?" he asked.

My cheeks flushed. "Davon? That's private. I can't believe you would ask me such a personal question."

"Huh? I'm sorry. Are you embarrassed to say how long you've been his girlfriend?"

My mouth hung open. My mind was clearly in the gutter. This man had me in a haze, thinking about the idea of being with him in every way. I completely took his question and allowed my mind to run with it.

"I'm sorry, I misunderstood."

His forehead creased. "What'd you think I meant?

I fanned away his follow-up to my distracted thoughts. "Rodney and I have been together for five years. We met here at the airport. He used to work for TSA, but quit after he started managing security for a friend who opened a night club."

Davon's forehead wrinkled again as if he was working out his thoughts. I wished he'd go ahead and let it out versus staring at me while he silently chewing his food. I cleared my throat and decided to draw it out of him. I couldn't take his silence any longer.

"What're you thinking about?" I asked. "You looked like you spaced out for a second there."

"I just wondered if you were engaged to him? Or maybe there was a wedding that didn't happen for one reason or another." He shook his head. "I don't mean to be intrusive, but after I heard you say how long you've been with him... I couldn't see myself being with a woman I loved for five years and not wanting to marry her. He should know if you're the one by now. Unless maybe you don't want to marry him?"

I opened and closed my mouth. He had struck a nerve and while I probably shouldn't be offended, I was. Yes, Rodney should know if he was ready to marry me. It wasn't like we were still in our twenties. I just turned forty this year and I wanted a family. Everything he said rang true and it hurt like hell. My shoulders rose and sank, as I released a breath.

"Davon, this has been nice, but I think I should get back to work." I pushed my chair back and placed my napkin on the table. "Thanks for lunch."

Davon followed my lead and came around the table, he offered his hand to me to help me from the chair. I took it but didn't look at him. "Wait, can we walk back together? Let me just gather the food, pay the bill, and then we can go."

"Davon, I don't know. I think maybe this was a bad idea." I smoothed out my skirt and nodded. "Yeah, actually, I shouldn't have agreed to join you. I'm going to go ahead and get back. If you don't mind, I think I'll take this walk alone."

I started towards the exit and I could hear Davon's tentative steps behind me. I slowed and turned around to face him just as he made it to the entrance of the restaurant.

"I'm so sorry. I had no right to get all up in your business the way I did. I like you. Yes, I know I don't know you well, but there's something about you. It's like I said there's just—"

"Chemistry," I said, cutting him off. He smiled and I walked closer to him. "Look, everything you said is valid and of course, I've had those same questions about my relationship. It's just hard to hear someone else say it. Especially because—you were right. There's something here. It doesn't make sense and the timing is terrible, but there's just this magnetic pull between us."

There, I'd finally admitted it. I couldn't believe the person I would make this confession to would be the last person I should be sharing this with. It felt good though. It was a freeing release and the twinkle in his eyes let me know he shared the sentiment.

He took a step back and rubbed his hands together. "I'm gonna throw something out there, and you tell me if you're game."

I gave him a quizzical look. I feared what he was about to say, but I also got butterflies in my stomach as the anticipation built. "Okay, I'm listening… nervous, but I'm listening."

"I'll be gone for a year with this job. If when I come back, we are both single, maybe we can give us a shot. What'd you say? And I promise, if things work between us, it won't take me five years to know if I want you to be my wife. It might not even be one year."

The heat in my belly rushed to my face when he said that. Not because I didn't think it could happen for me, but because I knew it wouldn't take much for me to fall for this man. My heart already jumped each time I was near him. Destined. That's the word that came to mind whenever he came around. And I couldn't wait to see what could happen if an opportunity was presented for Davon and me to date.

He held out his hand so we could seal the deal with a handshake, just as the restaurant's hostess appeared.

"Is everything okay?" she asked.

"Uh, yeah, just waiting on this young lady to shake on our agreement," Davon said, his eyes never leaving mine.

"Handshake? Why not seal it with a kiss? You're standing under the mistletoe," she said pointing up.

Davon and I looked up, and back down at each other.

"Wait a second, this wasn't here earlier. Did you do this?" I asked him.

He threw up his hands to declare his innocence. I looked over at the hostess whose name tag read, Lisa.

"Oh, no this was all me," she interjected. "We were still putting up some decorations for our staff party later tonight. I just added this. I'm sweet on the guy who works baggage claim. He's supposed to grab lunch here later and I'm hoping he'll linger here for a second. Gotta shoot my shot."

I threw my head back in laughter, tickled by the irony of it all. Here I was with a man I'd longed to kiss but knew I shouldn't because it was wrong and now temptation was literally hanging over my head. I looked to Davon as his brow hitched and he started to smile. He licked his lips and moved in closer to me. "So, what do you think?

I blew out a breath and leaned in to give him my response. His soft lips met mine and I instantly melted into him. As his strong arms surrounded my waist, I ignored all of the reasons I shouldn't be kissing Davon and parted my lips slightly to invite his tongue to massage mine. When he did, it felt natural, as if our mouths were two distant lovers who'd finally found their way back home.

My body started to heat and tingle in places I hadn't wanted to let Rodney explore in months. Davon had me open, just as I knew he would and after today, I knew I wanted more of this man. More of this feeling his touch ignited inside of me. As we stepped apart, I allowed my mind to think of what next Christmas might look like with Davon by my side.

THREE

I kicked my heels off at the door of the condo and started towards the kitchen. It had been a long but rewarding day. I pulled open the fridge to grab a bottle of wine and poured myself a glass. When the first sip touched my lips, I thought about the sweet kiss I'd shared with Davon. Once I got back from lunch, Joelle was waiting for us and asked me to tell her everything. Neither of us told her a thing. Which proved to be hard, as Davon and I exchanged flirty glances until it was time for him to board the plane. As soon as he walked through the doors to the gangway, Joelle went into interrogation mode.

"Okay miss girl, spill it. He's boarded the plane now and I want to know what happened during lunch."

I cut my eyes at her but couldn't hide my smile. "We ate at that new place, Flavor 101, and it was really good. There are some leftovers in the fridge. We chatted for a bit. It was nice."

Joelle folded her arms over her chest. "Don't play with me. You act like I didn't see all the showing of the teeth and the sniggling going on when y'all stole glances at one another. Come up off the tea."

I sighed. "I'll tell you one thing and then you need to find some-thing to do. Okay?"

She nodded. "Yeah, yeah. Come on here. What happened? Y'all kissed, didn't you?"

"If you would just hush. We agreed to date this time next year if we are both single when he returns."

Her eyes ballooned and then she jumped up and down.

I grabbed her shoulders. "Stop before you go into labor."

She fanned herself and then pretended to cry, making whining noises as she dabbed at her eyes with a Kleenex. "Oh, Audie... I'm so happy for us."

"Us? What are you talking about?"

"You finally gonna have a good man and I'm not gonna have to hear about Rodney. Everybody wins."

I giggled all over again just thinking about her comment.

"What's so funny?" Rodney said, coming up behind me.

I hadn't even realized he was here. I guess the house being lit up should've been a clear indication. He always insisted on having every single light in the house on. It drove me wild. Especially since he wasn't helping to pay any of the bills around this place.

"Hello to you too," I responded. "Why didn't you take the chicken out? We were supposed to cook tonight and exchange one gift. Remember?"

He looked around the kitchen and groaned. "Dang, so you ain't bring nothing to eat? I figured you weren't gonna want to cook since you got off later."

I frowned. I had told him earlier to take the chicken out of the freezer when he woke up so it would be thawed by the time I got home. He couldn't cook, so the least he could've done was to make sure what I needed was ready to go once I arrived.

"Ro, I texted you earlier to remind you, and you said you would take care of it."

He ran a hand across his scruffy face and sighed. "My bad. I got distracted and forgot. You wanna do AtlEats?"

I nodded. "Yeah. I guess so. Since it's clear we won't be having the Christmas Eve dinner we'd planned earlier this month."

"Cool. If you get—"

"Seriously? Come on, Rodney. I just got off work and you've been here this whole time. You're the reason we won't be having a home-cooked meal tonight. The least you can do is order us something while I take a shower."

He groaned and folded his arms across his chest. "You being mad difficult, babe. You actin' like I don't work too. And workin' evenings, at that. You know what tho'… don't even sweat it. I'm gonna take one for the team and order us some food."

"Gee, thanks," I muttered. "What would I do without your generosity? You're a real saint, Rodney."

I rolled my eyes and stomped into the bedroom. I hadn't even gotten into the door good and we were already arguing. I unzipped my skirt and let it fall to the floor. As I started working the buttons of my blouse, I noticed a small gift box wrapped in gold paper on the nightstand. I covered my mouth to keep from screaming.

It was a little larger than a ring box, but there was ample room to hide a smaller box inside. But if there was an engagement ring inside, why would he just leave it out like this? I froze in place as a thought ran through my mind. What if he was standing…no kneeling behind me, just waiting to propose. I closed my eyes and turned around slowly. I took a deep breath and opened my eyes to see no one there. I shook my head and chuckled at my foolish thoughts.

I walked over to the nightstand and stopped short. There wasn't a nametag on it, but it was on my side of the bed and we did say we'd exchange one gift tonight. So, I had to assume this was meant for me. But what was inside the box?

If this were an engagement ring, he may have planned to hide it, but got distracted when I walked into the condo. I backed away from the box and headed into the bathroom to shower. As soon as I started the water, I heard Rodney enter the room.

"The food will be here in about thirty minutes. I ordered from the Thai spot we like."

"Okay," I said coming out of the bathroom.

"Oh, I thought you were in the shower already," he said, rubbing the back of his bald head. He gave me a once over and smirked. "I see you got on the sexy bra and panty set I got you last Christmas. Those your festive panties now?"

"It's not the holidays without them." I walked over to him and put my arms around his neck. I figured I needed to shift the energy so I could ask about the present. "Listen, I got home and we got into it over something petty, and that's not how I want us to end this night. I think we both had a long day and brought that energy into our relationship. It's Christmas Eve. Let's start this over and try to be kinder to one another. I apologize for getting frustrated with you. So, tell me, how was your day?"

He lifted me off the floor and kissed me before returning me to the carpet. "I'm sorry too, bae. My day was banging. Boss hooked me up with more hours. I went in a few hours earlier to help set up for the Christmas joint. They doing the pre-party tonight and the main event tomorrow. It's supposed to be hella celebs there, so I'm gonna be super busy."

I nodded and turned my back to him, as I tried to hide my agitation. I know he wasn't saying what I thought he was saying. "What time are you supposed to be there tonight and tomorrow? You're still planning to come with me to my parents, right?"

He puffed out a breath and I knew he was about to give me some weak apology. "Babe, I got to get this money. He offering overtime and holiday pay."

I shook my head. So much for my attempt to get us in a

positive mood. He had ruined any positive vibes I might have conjured up. "Are you serious? You told me you were gonna take off and we were gonna cook dinner together, decorate the tree, and open at least one gift tonight. Then tomorrow we told my parents we'd come there."

He threw up his hands. "Man, don't start this, Audie. We didn't promise your parents anything—you did. And you know good and darn well that no one is going to miss me at your parents' house. Your dad doesn't even like me, and your mom only puts up with me because she loves you. Trust me when I say, it's not gonna be an issue if I'm not there."

I paced back and forth in front of him. "You know what, you're right. You're so freaking right. I don't know why I bothered. You don't need to come with me tomorrow and we don't need to celebrate tonight. You just gave me the best gift —clarity. And I'm glad I'm finally seeing your type of present for what it is. This… this is done. I don't even know why we hung on to this for as long as we did, but let's stop pretending we are something we aren't."

He chuckled. "I don't even know what you're saying. Give it to me straight."

"It's over. You can take what little you have here with you and be out. Let's do each other a favor, and give each other the gift of freedom." I turned my back to him and walked back towards the bathroom. I couldn't look at him anymore. "This so-called relationship is way past the expiration date. I'm tired of all the arguing and the lack of consideration for my feelings. Let's be done."

He clicked his teeth and grunted. "And to think, I had got you this little ring joint out the lost and found. Guess you don't want this promise ring, huh?"

I swung around and stared at him like he was the dumbest man alive. I walked up to him and cocked my head to the side. "I'm sorry, did you say you were about to give me a promise ring? And more importantly, one you found in the lost and found at the nightclub?"

"Yeah. Some idiot lost it during their turnup. It's nice too. I was gonna promise my love to you, but you over here saying it's over. Then cool. I can take it back to the club."

I folded my arms across my chest and smirked. "You should. Cause I'm not interested in wasting any more time with you or wearing a ring to promise... promise what? Another five years? Just take that Cracker Jack ring and get out."

He groaned. "Oh, you tryin' to play me? I was promisin' my time to you and you ready to throw it all away, huh? You know how many girls be jockin' for my attention in the club? Beaucoup, baby... but I bring all of this home to you." He lifted his shirt and ran a hand down his somewhat ripped abs. "You better be sure before you turn me away."

I looked him over and burst out laughing. What in the world was I doing with this clown? "You know what, please feel free to split my time between whomever you've been creeping with and the long line waiting for you at the club. Cause I'm good."

I headed back to my awaiting shower. I didn't want to hear anything else he had to say. The water had been running so long, it was probably losing steam. I stepped inside, happy to feel the warmth of the water against my skin and not caring if Rodney was still in the room or if he'd left altogether. I hoped for the latter.

I heard him enter the bathroom and wiped my hand across the steamy glass door to see him leaning inside of the door frame. "Audie, baby, I'm gonna let you cool off. I'm sure you'll be more relaxed after the shower and then we can get back to doing us. Just like always."

I shook my head and turned my back to him so I could finish my shower. I frowned as I reflected on those last three words he said – just like always. I wanted to do any and everything but go back to what Rodney and I had done for all these years. There was nothing left here and hadn't been for a while. I had wasted so much time on him, and I couldn't figure out what it was about him that made me hold on for as long as I did.

As I worked a good lather over my body, I resolved that today was indeed a new day, and now more than ever, I was ready to move on from this idiot. I turned off the water, wrapped a towel around my body, and stepped out of the bathroom. A knock on the front door interrupted my thoughts. I walked into the living room where Rodney stood with his back to me as he pulled plates from the cabinet.

"Baby, you got out just in time. The food is here and ready to be served," he said.

"Don't worry about plates," I said.

"Cool. I'm down to eat from the container," Rodney said and laughed. He returned the plates and turned to me with a huge grin on his face. "Ain't nobody trying to wash dishes anyway."

"Rodney, I meant what I said back there… this is over. We tried and failed to make this work. You paid for the food so you can take it with you, or I can give you half if you like."

"Gonna pay me for half of the food? That's what we on?" he spat. "I can't believe you even comin' at me like this."

He looked over at the table where the food sat and scowled as he stomped towards it. I could tell he was thinking about doing something stupid. "Rodney, before you think about knocking or throwing that food to push your point, think again."

He punched the air and grunted. "Yo, you're buggin'. Throw food? That's what you think of me? Can you please stop trippin'? Look, this is what I need to happen right now. Let's eat. Then we gonna open gifts like we planned and then we're gonna make love. Let's kiss it out and get over it like we always do. Period. Ain't nobody got time to play games with you."

"You know what Rodney, no... you can keep your "just like always" mentality because I'm not doing another five years of this. Scratch that, I'm not doing another second."

He ran a hand down his face. "What do you want from me, huh? You about to throw everything we have away?"

I dropped my head and I released a somber laugh. "What Rodney? What do we have? No wait, I'll tell you. All we have is a five-year investment with no return and I'm over it."

"You know what your problem is?" He stopped in front of me, wagging his finger as if he was about to make some strong argument. "You want to compare us to other couples and it's caused friction in our relationship."

I stepped closer to him and shook my head. "No, Rodney. Our issue is a lack of love. Lack of interest in each other. And neither of us has done a thing to make it better. This is not how love should feel...or at least not to me. We should both want better."

He pulled out a chair at the table and sighed. "Tell me this, how is it that we've been together all this time, and you're saying what I give you is not love?"

I looked at the wall and sighed. "Remember when you were a little kid and you couldn't sleep on Christmas Eve? All you could do was think about all of the great gifts you would receive. Then as you got older, you better understood God's gift, the importance of family, and the joy you get from watching family and friends unwrap their presents—that's what love should feel like. I believe love should always feel like I'm opening a new gift. It should be special, and this doesn't have that effect anymore."

He frowned. "What are you talking about?"

"Love is happiness. Love is peace. Love is affection. None of that lives here anymore. We aren't happy and haven't been in a long time. This—us—it's no longer bringing me joy. Can you honestly say you're happy?"

"Man, keep the food, and keep this conversation. I ain't hungry no way." He stood up and leered at me for a second before he started towards the door. "You're gonna regret this. Do you know that? I'm out of here. I'll come back for my stuff later."

He marched towards the door and snatched his keys off the coffee table on his way out. As reality set in, I stopped him before he could leave. "Rodney, wait..."

He turned around with a huge grin on his face. "I knew you'd come to your senses. And I forgive you."

I walked over to him and took the keys out of his hands. He started pulling his shirt over his head. I took a step back and sighed.

"What the hell?" he said, as he saw what I was doing.

"I'll bring your things to you. I wanted to make sure I got my house key." I said and held it up. "You won't be needing it anymore.

He pulled his shirt back down and sucked his teeth. I walked over to the table in the entryway to grab my keys and return his back to him. He opened the door and held up his hand. "Keep it. You'll be back for more than just dropping off my things."

I shook my head and closed the door on him and our raggedy relationship. I started towards the bedroom to throw on some pajamas when there was another knock on the door. I looked through the peephole and sighed. I knew it had to be Rodney, and I hoped he wasn't coming back to start some drama.

"What is it? I'm not in the mood for any mess." I said through the door.

"Can you please let me in so everyone in the building ain't hearing my business?" Rodney pleaded.

I groaned. "Hold on a second." I padded back into the

bedroom and slipped into some sweats. I took my time returning to open the door because I didn't feel pressed to let him back in. I didn't want to drag out the inevitable.

I cracked the door and he held up his hands before I opened it the rest of the way for him to enter. I took a few steps back to let him inside. "Okay, what is it?"

"Can we please sit down?" he asked, as he moved to the living room. I gestured towards the sofa and he plopped down.

I sat on the arm of the loveseat with my arms folded. "Say what you need to say? I'm tired and don't feel like talking about this anymore."

His shoulder lifted and he released a breath. "I'm sorry for how I reacted to you saying it's over. I know I ain't been doing enough to keep you happy or to build us. I ain't tried or cared to step it up. I got comfortable and you ain't deserve that. I'm not trying to reconcile our relationship or anything, but after all these years I figured... we can't end it like this."

I frowned. "Okay. So, what are you proposing?"

His mouth twitched and he burst out laughing. "One thing I ain't proposing is for you to put on that ring from the lost and found box. That ain't go over well, huh?"

I rolled my eyes, but couldn't help but smirk. "No, it did not, and make sure you take that hot ring out of here. I don't want to be an accessory to your crime."

He nodded. "I got you. What do you say we at least break bread this last time? The food is here and afterward, I can grab my some of my stuff and be out."

My lips twisted and my head cocked to the side as I said, "Okay. Cool, but you're gonna eat, grab your stuff, and leave. Don't be thinking we are gonna break anything else off one last time."

"Please, you're the one who needs to keep her hands to herself. I'm good." He laughed and reached out to hug me.

His mouth lowered to my ear and he said, "'Preciate you and sorry for flipping on you."

I stepped out of his embrace and nodded. "Yeah okay. Just come on so we can eat."

He rubbed his hands together as he walked over to the table. "By the way, I'm lying and I meant everything I said. I just wanted to grub real quick before I went to work."

"Is that right?" I said with a laugh and punched him in the arm. "I believe it."

As we walked back towards the kitchen, I thought about the constant turmoil we experienced in our relationship, and how all it took for us to find peace, was to finally decide to let each other go. I took the plates down and smiled.

Looks like Joelle was right. The best gift he could give me was freedom.

FOUR

The Day Before Thanksgiving, 2019

I rushed through the customers in my line. I didn't want anything to interfere with my reunion with Davon. His flight from Colorado was scheduled to come today, which I found out from my social media stalking. He was originally supposed to return next month, but it looked like he was coming back earlier and I was here for it.

In my thorough review of his page, it looked like he was still single. I hoped this was the case because I was available and ready to dive into some unrestricted flirtation. He had a few photos with a woman named Laila tagged in them. I attempted to do some light snooping on her page, but her privacy filter put a stop to my plans. I could only hope she was a close friend. I guess I would find out soon enough.

I had to remind myself that social media doesn't always present a person's reality. I never broadcast my relationship on my page. The only way anyone who didn't know me would know my relationship status would be if they asked. There weren't many photos of us on my page anyway. Over the years, Rodney and I started taking fewer photos and date nights were more of a surprise than a plan. At any rate, I was sure Davon didn't take as much time to explore my page as I had his because the last time he checked, I was still with Rodney.

"I see you let your hair down today," Joelle said, taking her hand to tuck a strand behind my ear. "It looks nice. I love when you wear it parted down the middle like that. It shows your face more."

I pressed out my long tresses and applied bronze shimmer powder to my face. I didn't usually wear a lot of makeup, but I applied mascara, eyeshadow, and a light, pink lip gloss. I wanted to enhance my features and I hoped he would see me and want to sweep me off my feet. Of course, I was well aware that I might be living in a fantasy world with these thoughts, but a girl could dream.

"Thanks, girl. I can't wait to see him." I twisted the charm on my necklace while I looked at the exit awaiting Davon's return. I took a deep breath and started to chew on my thumbnail.

"Don't be so anxious," Joelle said. "He's already let you know he's interested and now—"

"I just have to wait and see if he's single too." I sighed and shook my head. "I think I played this wrong, you know? I should've gone ahead and got his number, or sent him a private message to say I wasn't with Rodney anymore. I just… I thought it made sense to take the time to be single. I was in a relationship for five years. I needed to regroup and make sure I wasn't rushing into anything."

Joelle smirked. "Okay, makes sense to me. Have you heard from your ex?"

"He hasn't called me and I haven't called him. After all those years, I guess I expected us to circle back to talk or fall into our old routine. But we both let go, and walked away with mutual respect."

Her head bobbed. "Good. I thought for sure he would try

to get back with you and you'd take him back. I'm glad to hear he hasn't come back around, and I'm proud of you for staying strong. I know you hate when I bring him up and figured if he had been in touch, you wouldn't have told me anyway. It's time for you to have someone in your life who compliments you."

My shoulders relaxed and I inhaled. "Thanks, girl. I'm happy. I know my worth. I feel rejuvenated, and most importantly, I'm ready to date. And hey, if Davon and I happen to fall in love—I won't be mad at all."

She squeezed my arm and turned away to help a customer. Today had been more hectic than usual which helped make the day go by faster. But I was still anxious for his return and easily distracted. I had looked up every hour for the past four hours as if I didn't know his flight was set to return at 2 o'clock. It was only noon and the closer we got to his arrival, the more manic I felt.

"Okay. I'm tired of you watching the door. Let's go grab lunch. Terri and Michael are here, so we can go together," Joelle offered. "Then you can relax your nerves and stop working on mine."

I chuckled. "Yeah, okay. We might as well go. It's not like I can concentrate on anything anyway."

We walked to the food court and grabbed two cobb salads. I added grilled chicken to mine while Joelle got shrimp. We chatted and chewed, but I still couldn't get my reunion with Davon off my mind.

I tapped my fork against the bowl and sighed. "How's my baby doing?"

"Mazey is fine, but don't act as if you care. You know your mind is deep in the world of Davon," Joelle joked.

"I can't help it," I whined. "I spent all this time making sure I was truly ready to move on and I am, but what if I made a mistake. What if taking time for myself means I missed an opportunity? I should've told him I was single and that I was taking some me-time. My silence may have left him open to meet someone new."

Joelle's shoulder lifted. "Okay, it doesn't make sense to worry about what you don't know. Okay? And besides, you stalked his page and said you didn't see any clear indication of a girlfriend."

I nodded as I checked my watch. "Yeah. You're right. Are you ready to head back?"

"You hardly touched your salad. Take a few more bites and then we'll go."

I smirked. "You're such a good mommy, Joelle."

She rolled her eyes and chuckled. "Honey, hush. Hurry up and eat so we can go."

We arrived back at our gate just in time to see that Davon's flight was coming in ahead of schedule. I checked my watch and frowned. "Girl, his flight is gonna be early. What the heck? I almost missed him."

Joelle snorted. "Girl, he's gonna arrive in like thirty minutes. How is that you about to miss him? Calm your butt down."

I pinched her arm and she winced. "Whatever. I need to go freshen up my makeup and make sure I don't have anything in my teeth."

"And take a few deep breaths while you're in there too. You need to relax." She tilted her head to the side and gave me a knowing look before leaving me standing there.

I rushed to the restroom to take a look in the mirror. I raked my fingers through my hair and dabbed on some cherry lip-gloss. I then spritzed my neck and wrist with some perfume before I smoothed a hand across my lavender and royal purple uniform. I inhaled deeply and released a breath. Any minute now, Davon would be walking through the doors outside of my gate. Hopefully alone.

I stepped out of the restroom and headed back to my work station. I paused as I saw Davon coming out. I heard my phone ringing but didn't bother to answer it. I increased my speed and nearly ran over to my area, hoping to get more than a glimpse of him.

"Davon," I called out. He didn't hear me so I rushed over in his direction and tried to get closer to him, so I could try again. My heart pounded against my chest and my breath grew ragged as I quickened my steps. I stopped short as the full picture came to view. Davon wasn't alone, and not only was he with someone—she was the girl from the photos online. Dang, it.

My phone started to buzz again, and I sighed as I reached into my purse to retrieve it. Before I could even say anything, Joelle's voice filled my ears.

"Girl… where the heck are you? It's some chick—"

"I know. I saw. She's the one who was tagged in the photo on his page." I sighed. "I should've reached out to him as soon as I told Rodney we were done. I waited too long."

"Uh-yeah, enough of that. He hasn't left yet. He's looking around now. Probably looking to see if you're here," she said.

"I don't know why," I mumbled. "He's got somebody. Well, I guess that's settled."

"Ma'am, I see your butt over there looking defeated, but I got a trick for your behind," Joelle said. There was a pause and then, I heard, "Davon, hey. Who're you looking for, Audie?"

I groaned. Oh no she didn't. Davon turned his head in my direction and waved. Yes, she did. I had no choice but to head over there now to see him and his new boo.

FIVE

I licked my lips and made tentative steps in his direction. I looked over at Joelle and she smiled, which I'm sure she was doing to reassure me, but I was a ball of nerves. The grin on his face was warm and welcoming, but the leech of a woman clinging to his arm was not. If she were any closer, I'd think she was a life-size tattoo on his body.

"Hey, welcome back," I said, as I stood in front of him.

"Thanks. Wow, you look great. It's been a while since I saw you with your hair down. You look beautiful," he said. He complimented me in front of his date, which I hoped meant Laila was not his woman. Maybe she was just a friend.

Joelle leaned in and muttered, "It would look better if you smoothed out those flyaway hairs. Yes, you ran, but you don't need to look like it."

"Thank you, Davon," I said, cutting Joelle a look. I attempted to smooth out my hair and took a step in his direction. "It's good to see you."

"Ahem, aren't you going to introduce me, Davon?" the clinger asked.

I resisted the urge to roll my eyes and forced a smile as I looked in Laila's direction. She didn't need to know I was well aware of her name and was more interested in finding out who she was to him.

"Oh, my bad," he said, as he turned to her. "Audie, this is my friend and client, Laila. She's the Creative Director for ColorArts Inc. The new customer I mentioned."

Friend and client? Okay, that's a good sign. I exhaled in relief and extended my hand to her. "Hello, nice to meet you. I'm Audrienne. Everyone calls me, Audie."

"And I'm Joelle," she called from behind the counter. "So, did you two grow up together? Did you swipe right on his dating profile? How'd you meet?"

Laila reeled back and burst out laughing. She wagged a finger in Joelle's direction. "I heard all about you. The outspoken one. Well, to answer your question, Davon and I have known each other for years. Recently, we started to chat again when I identified him as a consultant for the new software we want to implement at my organization. With each conversation, I recalled just how good Davon and I were together. It was like no time had passed between us. Once he moved to Denver for this project, I got to test my theory and was in awe of our chemistry. It's like we were perfectly matched."

I looked over at Davon to see his reaction to Laila telling us how they met. He was frowning. Another indication that she wasn't his woman. I wondered why he didn't correct her or stop her from going on the way she did. I would ask him about that later.

"Oh, wait, let's back it up. Davon, you been talking about me and Audie?" Joelle gestured between us. I released a breath. I felt like Laila was making comments to get a reaction out of me. This made me wonder what he said about me, and for once I was glad to have Joelle's interrogation skills handy.

Laila interjected herself. "He told me there were two gate agents who always made him feel welcomed when he had to travel. He said I was going to love you because you're outspoken, like me."

Joelle's brows lifted. "Uh-huh… and what did he say about Audie?"

Her face scrunched up as she looked over at me. "Not much. He mostly compared me to you."

Davon scowled and started to say something, but Laila cut him off. "Anyway, it's good to meet both of you." The tight-lipped smile she wore was fake and confirmed my thoughts—this chick was messy.

I smirked and looked from her to Davon. "So, are you in Atlanta on business?"

She shook her head. "No, but I was having so much fun with my guy here, I wasn't ready to let him go. I decided to grab a ticket and come hang for a bit."

"Oh, are y'all dating? Davon, you finally got you a lady?" Joelle pried.

Davon chuckled. "Oh, how I missed you, Joelle. You dropped that bun out of the oven so you could make room to get into this Da-von. Get it? It's like a play on words cause my name is Davon but I'm saying it like oven."

I snorted and joined him in a hearty laugh. I had missed his cheesy jokes. On impulse, I touched his arm and he grabbed my hand. I caught Laila eyeing me and straightened up, as I released his hand. I looked over at Joelle and she was grinning from ear to ear.

"Now see, it makes no sense for both of you to be so corny," Joelle said pointing at us.

Laila put her hand on Davon's chest before she gave Joelle a wary look. "I apologize for Davon. My man is corny as hell, but I love him anyway."

Davon cringed and started to say something again, but just like the time before, Laila jumped in before he could respond. "But look at his adorable face, how can you not give him a pass."

Joelle gave me a look and returned her attention to Laila. "Well, I'm not apologizing for Audie. She's my friend and colleague, but she doesn't belong to me and I'm not claiming her love of cheesy jokes."

I looked Davon over and smiled. "Sorry, but I think he's pretty funny."

"Hmm, you sure do, huh?" Laila said. She gave me an askance look and offered up a half-smile before I looked away.

"Thank you, Audie. I'm glad someone appreciates my humor." His eyes lingered on me and I didn't turn away. I looked deep into his eyes and searched for an answer to my questions. Was he still free? Did he still want to be with me?

"Davon, do you have a second?" I said, not knowing where my voice or nerve came from. I was an introvert and asking a man, presumed to be taken, to join me in a private conversation was a bold move for me.

"Sure," he said as he stepped toward me.

"I'm sorry. Audie, right? Davon and I need to get going," Laila said, though it was clear I wasn't speaking to her. "Remember, I have that Zoom meeting in a few hours, so I need to get situated for the call. But hey, do you have Audrienne's number?"

Funny, she just acted like she didn't know my nickname but now she was calling me by my first name. Then she sat here and lied about a meeting, which was right after she told me she wasn't here for work. With everything she did and said, I had to hope she wasn't his woman. Even if we couldn't be together, surely, he didn't want someone who brought drama to come into his life. It was cool though; all she did was set things up in my favor.

He looked turned off by her constant interruptions and overly aggressive antics. I would just continue to keep it cute and let her push him away with her over the top behavior.

"No, he doesn't," I interjected and moved closer to him,

prepared to exchange numbers. Davon and I should've done this a while ago, so her interference helped my plight. "Davon, here, I can give you my number now or you can give me yours, so we can talk. Maybe you'll have some time tonight?"

I didn't want to come across as desperate, but a huge part of me felt like if Davon and I didn't have this conversation now, Laila would continue to interfere with us connecting. And from the looks of it, she was determined to make sure I didn't get any alone time with him.

"Wow, Davon. I'm surprised you don't have your *favorite* gate agent's number. Guess you two need to reevaluate this friendship. Ain't that right, Audie?" Laila said. She crossed her arms and wore a satisfied grin. It was official, I couldn't stand her.

I ignored her and looked at Davon, who appeared to be agitated. At any rate, we both recited our numbers and said our goodbyes. I watched them walk away and turned my attention back to Joelle.

"Well, that didn't go as expected," I said and frowned. "I probably shouldn't have even bothered to ask to speak with him alone. He's taken now, or at least that's the vibe she's promoting."

She held up her hand to silence me. "Hold up, I'm just gonna stop you right there. He didn't say she was his woman. Yeah, she's claimed the hell out of him, but until you hear him say it, don't count yourself out. You see how he scowled when she said my man and tried to downplay whatever he's shared about you? I think he didn't want to put her on blast in front of us, but I bet you he gives her an earful in the car."

My lips twisted and I shrugged. "I guess. Well, anyway, let me go put my stuff in the locker so I can get back to work."

I opened my locker in the employee breakroom and started to put my purse inside when my cellphone buzzed. I swiped the screen to unlock it, and smiled at the message waiting for me.

This is Davon. Sorry about Laila. It's about time I got your number though. Lol. Talk to you soon.

Audrienne: Saving your number now. Great seeing you and can't wait to catch up.

I saved his number in my phone and held it against my chest. I knew I needed to keep my expectations low, but seeing him and knowing there was a chance for us to be together, it was hard not to let my mind run wild. I touched my lips reminiscing about the first time we kissed. I wanted so badly to do it again, but he brought Laila with him and she put a halt to all of my plans. My phone chirped again, breaking me away from my thoughts.

Davon: Same here. Oh, and I hope it's not too forward for me to say you looked nice today.

Audrienne: Not too forward at all. Thanks. You're nice to look at too.

I smiled and tucked my phone away. Regardless of what happened, at least I chose myself over the dead-end relationship I had with Rodney. I'd be lying though if I said my hope was not for me to end up with Davon and that he'd be everything I've been missing and more. I could only hope what Joelle said was true.

SIX

No new messages. This was not how I expected to start my morning. As I padded downstairs to fix breakfast, my mind immediately went to Davon and Laila. I was disappointed he hadn't called or texted me last night, and I had hoped to wake up to find a message from him. No such luck. I feared Laila was to blame and I didn't even want to think of all the ways she could've distracted him.

I shook my head and sighed. I needed to know their relationship status, and I wanted to hear it from Davon. I knew I could call and ask him, but if she was his woman, I didn't want to cause him any problems by reaching out.

As if on cue, my phone started to ring. I groaned. Of course, it would be upstairs in my bedroom. I took the stairs, two at a time, in an attempt to catch my phone before it stopped ringing. I rounded the corner at full speed and instantly regretted it.

"Ugh!" I screamed as my baby toe hit the sharp edge of the bedroom door. I hopped the rest of the way over to the bed so I could grab my phone off of the nightstand. The ringing stopped by the time I reached it.

I sighed and sat on the edge of the bed to rub my throbbing toe. I frowned and looked over at my door as if it assaulted me on purpose. With my free hand, I unlocked my phone to see if my pinky toe died for a cause or a scam call. It was my mom. I was hoping for Davon, but whatever.

"Hey. Good morning, Ma."

"Hey, baby. Did you remember that you're responsible for the macaroni and cheese casserole and cornbread dressing," she asked? "You know your father has got to have his dressing and cranberry sauce. I'm not trying to hear his mouth."

I chuckled. "Yes ma'am. I'm on it."

"Good. Your brother's over here digging in my greens but he needs to be minding the turkey he's frying."

I walked back downstairs and smirked at the thought of my brother. I wasn't surprised to hear he had ordained himself as the taste consultant over today's meal. He was always pregaming in the food before every family function.

"Oh, Lord. Does he know what he's doing? Momma, don't be letting Malik mess up the turkey." I put the phone on speaker and placed it on the counter as I moved about the kitchen.

She chuckled. "Chile, he and your father claim they got it under control. I got this Alexa thing you bought me turned on so I can tell her to call 9-1-1."

"Okay, good. I'm just about to get started. I had just finished eating breakfast when you called. I did my prep last night, so don't worry. I won't be late."

"No worries, baby. Your brother invited that Celeste over here. I don't know what they are doing. He keeps messing up and she keeps taking him back. It don't make no sense." A beat and then, "How'd it go with that fella you were telling me about? Are you inviting him over today?"

I smiled. My mom was my best friend and I told her everything. After I ended things with Rodney, she celebrated, and then when I told her about the charming stranger who frequented the airport, she was intrigued. She encouraged me to get to know him and said if I wanted to invite him over, so she could feel him out, I was welcome to do so. I wasn't gonna go that hard so quickly, but it would be nice to just get to talk to him today.

"I did see him, but he was with someone else, and I'm not sure who she is to him. He said she was a friend and colleague, but I don't know any real details about her. So, I guess the best way to answer your question is to say it didn't go well at all."

There was a brief pause before she said, "Well, did you ask him about her?"

I puffed out air as I walked over to preheat the oven. "No, I didn't get a chance to speak with him privately. If she was his woman, I didn't want to be disrespectful. He did send a text apologizing for her after they left, but I'm not sure if the apology was for her behavior, existence, or maybe both."

"Oh, she sounds interesting," she said with a chuckle. "Well, baby, why don't you send him a Happy Thanksgiving text and see how he responds? Maybe he'll give you a call."

I walked over to the refrigerator to grab my pans and nodded to myself. The holiday did give me an innocent excuse to contact him. "Good idea, Mom. I think I'm gonna do that. Thanks."

"No problem. You just make sure you tend to those dishes first before you get distracted with trying to text that man, here?"

"Yes ma'am," I said with a laugh. "See you in a few."

I leaned against the counter, as I waited for the oven to alert me to its readiness. My eyes landed on my phone as I thought about sending Davon a message. I knew my mom was right. I needed to focus on getting my sides in the oven before I fixated on what to include in my text, but my mind was already on him. I wondered if he was thinking about me and if he were with Laila and what were they doing.

The oven beeped and I put both of my dishes inside, set a timer, and then returned my attention to my phone. I picked it up and went back and forth in my head on whether I should text or call. I mean, we were adults and I know I would've wanted a call. Then again, what if Laila was right there next to him—in his bed. Ugh, that could be awkward and unnecessary trouble for him. I put the phone down and closed my eyes, as I tried to get my thoughts together.

"Oh, shoot!" I screeched, startled by the shrill ringing of phone. I held my chest as I reached for it. I frowned when I saw the unknown number pop up. I sent the call to voicemail and walked over to the sink to wash dishes when it started to ring again. I turned on my heels to look at the screen and noticed it was the same number. I picked it up this time but didn't say anything. I wanted to see if it was an automated caller.

"Hello? Audrienne?" the caller said.

"May I ask who is calling?" I responded. The voice sounded familiar and I hoped it was not who I thought it was.

"This is Laila. I wasn't sure if anyone answered. All I heard was dead air. I called a few seconds ago, but I got your voicemail and thought I'd try again. I figured you might not answer. Most people don't answer unknown numbers."

"Hi. I was in the middle of cooking. Sorry I missed you. What's up?" I rolled my eyes. I wanted to curse myself out for answering this call. I knew I shouldn't have picked up. Not that I should be surprised, but she had a lot of nerve calling me. I didn't give her my number, but it was clear she made a mental note of it so she could bother me later.

"Oh, and you cook too, wow. I can't say the same. I'm not the domesticated type. I went to college and jumped right into my career. No time to learn the Suzy homemaker role. Good for you though," she said.

She tried it. I inhaled and pressed my tongue against the

inside of my cheek. I needed to hurry and get her off my phone before I snapped. "Laila, how may I help you?"

"Oh, not one for small talk," she said with a laugh. "My bad. I guess you did say you were doing something. I was calling to see if you planned to do some Black Friday shopping tonight. I thought maybe we could meet up."

I pursed my lips. I didn't understand this chick. She hadn't called to tell me to stay away from Davon. Or called to ask what my relationship was with him. She called because she wanted to hang out with me. Perhaps this was a ploy to find out more about me. I wasn't sure what her goal was, but I was about to find out.

"Is Davon with you?"

There was a brief pause before she responded. "No, he's at his place. Are you saying he needs to be present for me to call you?"

I nodded as if she could see me. "You'll have to excuse me, but wouldn't it make more sense? I don't know you, and I'm still getting familiar with him… so *yeah*, I don't see why we would kick it without him. Plus, you took it upon yourself to save my number and I don't recall asking you to call me."

I'm not the confrontational type, but she'd already tried it and I wasn't gonna sit here and wait on her next attempt.

She chuckled. "Okay, okay. To be honest, I just wanted to see who this woman was keeping Davon's attention. He just won't stop talking about you. The entire time we were in Denver, he kept bringing you up and showed me a few pictures of you on social media. Is that all your hair? He always ended up with the girls with long hair. Never mind. Anyway, you don't have to answer. So yeah, I just wanted to see what the fuss was about."

My eyes bugged out so hard, I felt like they would separate from my face altogether. "Are you and Davon in a relationship? Does he know you're calling me?"

"Oh, he didn't tell you about me?" she said, her tone mischievous.

I exhaled. She wanted me to go there. "It's like I told you, I'm still getting to know him. So, no, I don't know anything about you."

"Interesting. Well, I'll let him tell you about us. That is, if you two ever find time to chat on the phone. I'm planning to spend a lot of time with him while I'm here, so he'll be busy." She released a flirty laugh and I gritted my teeth. "But to answer your second question, no, Davon doesn't know I called you. We're all grown and I don't have to tell him who I call. And you shouldn't feel the need to act like a little girl and run and tell him I called you."

I shook my head. I'd had enough of her. "A little girl? Laila, I can't say it's been a pleasure. You take care. Or don't."

I hung up the phone and placed it on the counter. That raggedy heifer. It was clear Laila thought I was someone she could speak to any kind of way. Whatever her thought process was, she was wrong and I wouldn't have a problem showing her. None of her actions made sense to me. She must be his girlfriend or she was trying to be, right? Why else would she feel the need to interrogate me? Maybe she was jealous because he's shown interest in me and not her.

I picked up my cell and called Joelle, which I hated to do because it was Thanksgiving, but I needed her to pass some of her take-charge spirit over to me. I needed a pep talk.

"Happy Thanksgiving, Audie!" she yelled into the phone.

"Hey, girl. Happy Thanksgiving. Are you done cooking?"

She tittered. "You know good and darn well you don't care if I'm finished cooking. What's wrong? I can hear it in your voice."

I scrunched my nose. She knew me so well. "Yes, I did want to know about your cooking cause I'm hoping you're gonna save me some of your sweet potato pie. And yes, something is wrong. The heifer called me."

"Who? What heifer?" she asked.

"Laila, the chick who was with Davon at the airport. She called and asked if I wanted to go Black Friday shopping. And then, after I said I was cooking, she said she admired me for having time to learn how to be Suzy Homemaker. She said she was too busy with her career goals to be domesticated." I groaned as I paced back and forth in my narrow kitchen. "Anyway, I held my tongue but I wanted to go off on her."

I heard Joelle suck her teeth. "I don't know why you didn't give her an earful. Y'all ain't friends. She better back off."

"Exactly. Oh wait, and here's the best part. When I asked why she was really calling me, this wench said Davon won't stop talking about me and she wanted to see what all the fuss was about."

Joelle cackled. "Well, you know what this means? He must really like you and it's driving her crazy. It's the reason she's so pressed to see why it's you and not her who has Davon's attention."

"But that's the thing," I said as I hopped onto the counter to sit. "Is she bothered because she's after him? Or are they on a break and I'm in the way?"

"Look, there are two ways to find out. Take her up on her offer or you can call him and ask him yourself."

She had a point. I could go to the source or take advantage of Laila's attempt at pressing me for information and use the time to get to know everything about her and him. Of course, it would be easier to just call him, but if they are together and I called him—things could get messier. I didn't want to cause problems for them, and he had yet to call me, so maybe that was my answer right there.

Plus, if Davon could be friends with someone who likes to instigate drama, maybe this speaks to the type of person he is. And if we got together, would she ever leave us alone or would she continue to pursue him? Would I be okay with them remaining friends? I had a lot to think about.

"Are you still there?" Joelle called.

"Yeah, I'm here. Guess I'll call messy Laila back, but only if I don't hear from Davon by the end of the night."

"Just send him a 'Happy Thanksgiving' text. He'll call! Trust me. Davon has been waiting on this moment for a while. I say go for it."

"Yeah. My mom said the same thing. I'll think about it. Thanks, girl,"

When we hung up, I picked up the phone and scrolled to Davon's number. My finger hovered over the call button. I shook my head and decided to send a text instead.

Davon: Hey. This is Audrienne. Happy Thanksgiving!

I wrote, erase, read, and reread the text several times before hitting send. I was a novice when it came to being the hunter. My father always taught me to not chase after a man and allow him to pursue me. It was old fashioned and it was likely part of the reason I ended up with a dud like Rodney. He was used to women chasing him, and when I didn't fall all over him, it heightened his interest. Perhaps this was why Davon was interested in me.

I put the phone down and released a breath. Because now became the hard part, waiting to see if he'd text or call me back. I hoped he would because I needed to get to know him and his intentions. I'd much rather sit across from him than be bothered with that irritating Laila.

SEVEN

It had been five days since Thanksgiving. And still no word from Davon. He never called and never responded to my text. I decided against calling Laila. I wasn't in the mood for her negative energy. And I hadn't heard from Davon since that day at the airport, so it doesn't seem like he's as interested in me as I thought. I guess I should just move on, which sucked because I really liked him and believed he liked me too.

I stepped into my flats and went through the garage to get in my car. I smiled as the Emotions greeted me with one of my favorite Christmas songs, "What Do the Lonely Do At Christmas?" I turned up the volume and sang along. I loved this song. Yes, it was melancholy but it jammed, and at this moment it spoke to my soul.

Up until last year, Christmas was probably the one holiday where Rodney and I let go of the drama and just loved on one another. We never got too into exchanging gifts on Valentine's Day, and with our work schedules, it was hard for us to do activities as a couple. But we always managed to be with friends and family on Thanksgiving and Christmas. Last week marked my first Thanksgiving as a single woman.

My parents had each other. My brother had his girlfriend,

and then I was sitting there all alone. Yes, I had my family and I was grateful for their love and attention, but seeing everyone coupled up made me more aware of my single status. In a few weeks, I would have another first. After five years in a relationship, I would be spending my first Christmas alone. I sighed and turned the station. Suddenly, my favorite song started to feel sad.

My mind shifted to Davon. I looked down at my phone and sighed, I can't believe he didn't follow-up with me. I frowned as the phone started to ring. It was Laila. I rolled my eyes. This chick just won't go away. It was 7:30 a.m., way too early for her antics. I inhaled and clicked the "Accept" button. Here we go.

"Before you start in with your snarky comments, it's way too early in the morning and I'm not in the mood for any drama."

She chuckled. "I guess I deserved that. I did come at you wrong, and I apologize for my behavior. This is actually why I'm calling you now because I know I was out of character and felt the need to apologize."

"Oh, wow. This is so unexpected, Laila," I said, completely aware of how sarcastic I was coming off. "Remind me again, why do you keep calling me?"

"I love how you get to the point," she said with a rueful laugh. "I'm sorry. I was out of line. I know Davon likes you— a lot. And, it's just..."

Her words trailed off and I cleared my throat. I wasn't sure where she was going with this. "Thank you for sharing this with me, but I already know he likes me. Or I thought he did. What I don't know is why you felt the need to call me? I know it's not because you wanted to apologize."

She sighed. "Listen, are you free to talk in person? This is awkward, as is, and I'd like to be able to apologize and answer all of your questions, maybe over lunch or dinner?"

I shrugged. What the hell? "If this will get you to back off, sure, why not. I get off around 4:30 p.m."

"Great. So, um, yeah, we can meet around five. Just text me the location. My treat, of course. And I promise I'll be on my best behavior."

An hour later, I was standing in front of Joelle telling her about my call with Laila and my dinner plans.

"Dang. Why is she so pressed to talk to you in person?" Joelle asked. "Make sure you pack a shank or something."

I shook my head and turned to her. "I don't know. It's weird. All this over Davon and he hasn't even called me or returned my text. Maybe if I told her that she'd go away."

We stopped talking to assist two customers who approached the desk. As they walked away, we looked back at each other to resume our conversation.

"So where do you think y'all will go? I can't believe you're going through with this." Joelle said. "And do you want me to come just in case you need back up?"

I chuckled. "Back up for what? You're a nut. She don't want these problems."

Joelle guffawed. "Girl, bye. You're from the suburbs. You don't have hands."

"What?" I put my fist up and cocked my head to the side. "Don't be fooled. I can do some damage."

"Stop!" she said, holding her stomach as she laughed. She got so tickled that I could see tears coming out of her eyes.

I cut her a look and chuckled. "Whatever. Don't forget I spent summers with my grandma in Bankhead. The *real* Bankhead. The one rapper T.I. talks about in his songs. But anyway, no, I don't need you to be there. I'll be fine. She seems harmless enough. I'll probably pick something closer to the house. You know traffic is a bear for me at that time of day."

She nodded as she wiped at her eyes. "So, have you thought about what you'll say?"

"Say about what?" I frowned. "I'm not sure I follow."

Her face turned serious as she said, "I'm asking what you'll say if she confirms they're in a relationship."

I pursed my lips and sighed. "To be honest, I don't know and hadn't even thought about it. He and I agreed if we were both single, we'd connect and see if our chemistry went beyond the brief moments we spent together here. Then he hasn't even called, so I'm expecting him to be with her or anybody other than me at this point."

She smirked. "I hear you and I guess that's a good way to think about it. Might as well not worry yourself over what you don't know. Chin up. It's gonna be what it's gonna be."

I folded my arms over my chest and nodded. I grabbed my phone to see if there were any missed calls or texts from Davon and was disappointed once again. The only text I had was from Laila's annoying behind making sure we were still on for later because I hadn't confirmed a location with her yet. I sighed and texted her back.

"Was that him?" Joelle asked.

I shook my head. "I wish. He still hasn't said anything to me. It wasn't nobody but Laila asking where we were going since I hadn't responded yet."

Joelle cackled. "You're a mess. So, where are y'all meeting?"

I rolled my eyes. "Bobby Blues Diner. Just something quick and close to my house so I can get the heck on afterward."

"Ew, why didn't you choose a place where you can at least have some wine with dinner?" Joelle frowned and shook her head. "And the food there is mediocre."

I shrugged. "Yeah, I know, but their bacon burger is decent and I wasn't trying to spend all night in her company, so it'll do."

"Who knows, you may meet with her and you two forge a friendship. At the very least, you may find out some good tea on Davon." Her brows waggled as she smiled. "I say make the best of it and let her act a fool by herself. Don't give her any ammo to go back to him talking bad about you."

My lips twisted and I nodded. "I can't make any promises, but as long as she doesn't try it, I won't have to mollywop her behind."

Joelle's eyes widened and then she bent over in a fit of laughter. I rolled my eyes and turned to help a customer. I wasn't paying her any mind. I could fight. I just chose not to, and hopefully, I could make that choice tonight.

EIGHT

I rested my elbows on the metallic tabletop as Laila and I sat in awkward silence. I'd just arrived at the restaurant and she was already inside waiting for me. At least she was prompt. I tapped my fingers against the table and puffed out air as I tried to unwind to the soulful tunes coming out of the overhead speakers. The diner, true to its retro appearance, played some of Motown's greatest hits. Smokey Robinson's voice was a great distraction from the anxious thoughts running through my mind.

"So, this place is… interesting. Is this a local hang-out for you?" she asked. Her eyes roamed around the restaurant and mine followed.

The majority of the walls were white but there were three accent walls which were painted red, teal, and black to add a splash of color. My favorite part of the diner was the pastel portraits of Motown artists hanging around the restaurant.

"It's just a place to grab a quick bite. The owner, Bobby "Blues" Travis, used to play guitar for Mona Sims and the Soul Singers back in the day." I gave a half shrug. "I used to come here a lot back in the day. This is an after-hours spot.

Most people come here to eat greasy food that will soak up the effects of a long night."

She cackled. "I know all about those days. In my college years, I used to club with the best of them, but now, my knees and I are no longer able to get down like that."

I nodded and smiled. I couldn't help it because I could relate to what she was saying. The only difference might be, I still challenged myself to drop it low on occasion.

"Hi ladies, are you ready to order?" the young waiter asked.

"I'll have a bacon cheeseburger with fries, water, and would you please bring me a cup of coffee while I wait on my meal? Thanks."

I studied Laila while the waiter took her order. She was an attractive woman. Her russet complexion was flawless and her wide eyes were animated by her thick lashes. She had a face full of freckles, and a tiny space between her teeth which added some flavor to her smile. Her hair was a wild, free-flowing, bundle of deep waves, which from her bold approach to reaching out to me, seemed to fit her personality.

"I saw your nose turn up when I ordered the tuna melt. Is it not good? Should I change my order?" she asked.

That wasn't the only reason I had my face twisted but she didn't need to know. I shrugged. "Sorry, I don't know anything about the sandwich. I'm just not a fan of tuna. But anyway, how long have you known Davon?"

She chuckled and bit down on her lip. "That's right, you like to get to the point. I forgot. Listen, I know I got off on the wrong foot with you, but can we both please just let our walls down and be civil? I promise I'm not here to try you—again. I promise."

She held two fingers to her chest. I guess that was her way of saying scouts honor, so I sighed and allowed my shoulders to relax. "Okay, cool. I can try to be cordial, but you did put me on alert with your shady conversation. I'm not sure if you were trying to be funny, but since we don't know each other like that, I felt like you were coming for me."

Her head bobbed. She held her hand up and pinched her fingers together. "I was throwing a little shade the last time we spoke. I'm woman enough to admit it and I hope after we speak today, you'll see me different."

"Okay, so tell me, why did you want to meet?"

The waiter brought our beverages, giving her a second to collect herself and me a moment to try to fix my face. I was going to try my best to converse with her and leave the nega-tivity behind us—for now. But I'd be lying if I didn't say I already regretted my decision to meet with her.

"Um, so yeah, well thanks again for meeting me. This is awkward, so I'm just gonna talk and get everything out there. I want Davon."

My brow lifted. I wasn't sure how to respond or if I should just not say anything. I decided on the latter and kept my thoughts to myself.

"We grew up together in Colorado. Back then, I was into bad boys and as you can probably tell, Davon is not one of them." She smiled as she thought of him. "He used to like me when we were in middle school, but I wasn't paying him any attention because he was a bore. But in high school, I started to see the man he was becoming and realized how much I was missing out on."

I could see where this story was headed and used my coffee as a distraction. I grabbed the cream and sugar and poured it into my cup. I started to stir and look at any and everything but Laila. I felt like this was going to be a long story, and so far, I couldn't see how any of this had anything to do with me. I didn't want to interrupt her, but I wanted her to get to the reason why we were here.

"Sorry, I know this feels like I'm rambling especially to someone who likes to get straight to the point, so I'll jump ahead." Laila took a sip of her water before she continued. "I moved back to Denver after college, but our friendship has remained strong all these years. We've been there for each other in a lot of ways. If you know what I mean." Laila winked suggestively and laughed under her breath. "I recommended Davon's company to come partner with mine. As soon as he got back in town, I was there to welcome him home. The entire year I spent with him was like a movie. One of those romantic comedies. There were lots of dates, drinks, and passion. We made up for the lost time. Over time, we started to become intimate with each other. I guess one of those times we weren't very careful and now—."

My eyes narrowed as Laila ran a hand across her stomach. "I'm sorry, are you saying you're pregnant with Davon's baby?"

"You know what, excuse me, we shouldn't be discussing this. I haven't even told him yet. This is why I followed him to Atlanta. I just found out a couple of weeks ago and hadn't figured out how to tell him. I thought he was going to be in Denver longer. When he said he was taking an earlier flight back to Atlanta, I knew I needed to be here also. I just haven't found the nerve to tell him," she said, diverting her eyes across the room as she spoke.

I couldn't help but think this wench was lying. I didn't call her on it though because I wanted to see where this speech was going. I held up my hand and smiled. "I totally get it and I agree. You don't have to tell me anything else. As a matter of fact, you should probably go talk to him now instead of me."

I started to get out of my seat when she said, "I just want a chance to have a family with him."

I sat back down and folded my arms across my chest. I would play along and hear her out.

"Since his return to Denver, I thought maybe there was a chance we could finally get together. But even after all the dates and intimate moments we shared, he always ended up talking about you."

"Wow, not to be insensitive or anything, but what did he say about me?"

I couldn't help but grin because all I had been thinking about lately was him. Even though he hadn't called, something inside of me wouldn't let go of the idea of us. This entire year, I waited for him but I never got the chance to tell him I was still interested. I'm sure I have Laila to thank for that.

She rolled her eyes. "Why is it so important for you to know what he said? This is like the second time you asked or maybe it was your little friend."

I scoffed. "Perhaps if you told me, I wouldn't ask again. Just a thought."

She sighed. "He told me there was this girl he'd been feeling for a while but she had a boyfriend, and he was trying hard not to disrupt your relationship but he liked you. He also told me, you two agreed that if you both were single when he returned that you'd start dating."

My eyes widened. Now everything made sense. "I see, so when I asked to speak with him alone at the airport—"

"I cut you off because I knew as long as he thought you were taken, he wouldn't try to be with you and it would give me more time," she said. "And when we were in the car, and he was taking me to the hotel, I told him my phone was dead and asked to use his to check my email while mine charged. He let me and I saw where he'd texted you, which pissed me off because I didn't think it was right for him to apologize. I didn't do anything that required an apology." She smirked," Or well, I hadn't at the time. But since he tried to play me, I edited your number so he wouldn't have the right contact information."

"Wait, what? You did—wow." I was floored. "You are a real piece of work."

"Oh, and I stored your actual number under another name and blocked it. Just in case you got thirsty and tried to call him." Laila smiled triumphantly. "I know what you're thinking, but I had to do what was needed for me and my baby."

It all made sense now. I knew he was a gentleman and wouldn't press me since he wasn't sure if I was single, but for him to not reach out to me at all after I said I wanted to talk confused me. But now I understood. He hadn't reached out because he couldn't. Thanks to Laila. Maybe he had been hoping I would call him. Then when I only sent the happy holidays text, he probably thought I'd put him in the friend zone permanently.

"All right, ladies," the waiter said, as he returned with our plates. "We have a bacon cheeseburger and a tuna melt. Do you all need anything else?"

"I think we're good for now. Thanks," Laila said, smiling as if she hadn't just dropped a bomb on my lap.

Once he backed away from the table, I turned my attention back to her. "So, just to recap, you're pregnant with Davon's baby. You blocked and change my number in Davon's phone so we couldn't reach out to each other. And you did all of this because you need to tell him your pregnant and you want him to be your man. Did I miss anything?"

She clasped her hands together in front of her face and exhaled. "Look, I know this is a lot to take in but at least I'm coming to you with this. Plus, I've been here way before he started having this little crush on you and I'm about to have his child. I'm prepared to do whatever I have to do, to keep my growing family together. I'm not giving him up. You understand?"

I ran my fingers through my hair and chuckled. "I'm sure he doesn't know about your efforts to keep him from speaking to me. You've made it clear he doesn't know you're pregnant, but does he know how you feel about him? And I know you said you didn't want to continue the discussion, but when are you planning to tell him you're pregnant? I don't know you, but your sneaky tactics are making it hard for me to believe half of what you're saying. I hope for Davon's sake, that you're not lying just to trick him into being with you. You won't just lose a chance of being with him, but you'll lose him as a friend too."

A single tear traveled down her face, and she took a large bite of her sandwich. She covered her mouth as she chewed, "Excuse me, I'm an emotional eater. Or maybe it's because I'm eating for two now. But, no, I haven't expressed my feelings to him. He's either clueless or ignoring all the obvious signs. I've all but thrown myself at him and didn't think I needed to spell it out."

I hadn't even touched my burger. She had completely curbed my appetite with her big reveal. Selfish was the word that came to mind as I considered her actions. I needed to get out of here. I waved the waiter over. I said I would hear her out, and I'd heard more than enough crap for the day. This was beyond me and all I wanted to do was go home, call Davon, and tell him everything.

"Could I please have a to-go box? And the checks please," I asked.

He looked down at my untouched plate of food with raised brows. "Was something wrong with your meal?"

I shook my head. "I just wasn't as hungry as I thought I was. I'll just warm it up later."

He walked off to grab me a container and to close out our ticket.

"Laila, I appreciate your full disclosure. I know how you must feel because I've been waiting a year to tell Davon how I feel. I wish you all the best, and I hope you figure everything out. But, honestly, I'm over this conversation and I don't want to waste another second of my time talking to you when I could be speaking with Davon."

We sat in silence as we waited for the bill. Her eyes pleaded with me as she fingered her wavy hair. I knew she didn't want me to share what she had revealed, and I wasn't sure if I would honor her request. I didn't want to get in the middle of their drama. I just wanted the opportunity to connect with Davon.

She wiped her mouth and reached across the table to touch my hand. I looked down at her hand on top of mine, and back up to her face. She forced a smile and slowly withdrew her hand.

"Audrienne, thank you for listening, and I'm glad you understand because the reason I wanted to talk to you is that I wanted to ask if you'll give me at least until the week of Christmas."

I frowned. "Huh? What're you talking about?"

She licked her lips. "I'm asking you to allow me the time I need to tell Davon I'm pregnant and to see where we stand. And, it would be great if you hold off on telling him you're single. Please just give me until the week of Christmas to put my cards on the table and see where things could go. I mean, you just said it yourself, I need to put myself out there. I haven't yet and I need this time before I go back home. If not for me, do it for Davon's unborn child."

My lips formed a straight line and my eyes narrowed. I couldn't believe she would ask me to do this and then to say it was for the baby. It was just tacky. This chick should've gotten a job at Hasbro with all of the games she was playing. I couldn't believe she was trying to put a guilt trip on me, and I was annoyed with myself because it was working.

"It's only a few of weeks. This week is basically over—please just give me this. If he's not into me, I'll back off and just be his friend and leave it at that. You don't have to answer right now, but please just think it over and let me know tonight. Or tomorrow."

The waiter returned with my to-go box and our bills. Laila grabbed both tickets and headed to the register. She looked over her shoulder and smiled at me. "Just think about it. I know it's a lot to ask and you don't owe me anything, but I hope you'll be open to doing this for me and the baby."

As Laila headed to the register to pay for our meals, I sat there stunned at everything I'd just heard. I looked at my burger and rolled my eyes. I didn't even want it anymore. Who could eat with this type of proposal looming over their head?

Laila looked back at me and waved as she started out the door. Through the glass, I watched her get into the car and drive away. She looked lighter, and I guess she would since she unloaded all that was weighing her down on my shoulders.

NINE

Joelle cocked her head to the side, her eyes wide with indignation as she said, "I know the hell she didn't."

I put a finger in front of my lips and chuckled. "As much as I needed this laugh, you need to calm it down sis, before we get put out of here."

Her eyes widened as she folded her arms across her chest. "Uh-uh, you should've called me as soon as you left the restaurant. You knew I was gonna react accordingly. This moment is too large for a library response."

"What are you talking about now?" I asked. "Library response?"

She held a finger up to her lips. "You coming at me with the *shhh*, and telling me to use an inside voice on tea that deserves an outside voice. This is ridiculous and my reaction should match. You should've called me last night if you wanted me to be more reserved."

I sighed and I rolled my neck to release some of the building tension. "You're probably right, but all I did when I got home was get into the shower, pour myself a drink, and climb into bed."

"From the looks of it, you didn't sleep very well," Joelle

said. "You need to put a heating pad on your neck when you get back home."

"I barely slept at all. My mind was too busy thinking about Laila being pregnant and what this might mean for them. I don't know what I should do about this."

Joelle looked me up and down. "Wait a minute, I know you aren't telling me you're considering her request."

I groaned. "I went back and forth on it all night. Davon hasn't known about me being single for an entire year— what's a few more weeks?"

"Audrienne," she started, shaking her head. "You need to stop trying to talk yourself out of what you want. Screw her."

I ignored her and continued sharing my thoughts. "She said she's pregnant, but part of me thinks she's lying."

"I swear. This chick is unbelievable. Pregnant?" Joelle sucked her teeth. "I hope she's not out here lying on her womb. Who does that?"

I shrugged. "But hey, if it's meant to be, then it will be, right? Whether this is true for me and him, or him and Laila. I have to trust that if he and I are meant to be... nothing and no one will stop it."

Joelle staggered back and looked at me as if I had gunk on my face. "Audie... have you lost your mind? Ain't no way in hell, I'm letting you just bow out and let that Alex Forrest wannabe have him!"

"Who? Never mind." I rubbed the back of my neck and exhaled. "Okay. You've got to calm down, Joelle. If you stay hyped, then I'm going to follow suit. Take a breath or something."

"You're telling me, this chick took Davon's phone, and then edited and blocked your phone number so he couldn't call you. And last but not least, she told you she's pregnant with Davon's baby," she said with a hand planted on her hip. "And you want me to simmer down? You can forget it. I'm on a high boil at this point. And Alex was Glenn Close's character in *Fatal Attraction*."

I yawned and shooed her away. "Anyway, as I said, I don't think she's unbalanced or anything. I just think she's desperately in love with him and willing to do whatever it takes to have him. Something tells me she's into the type of love you see in those stalker movies on the Lifetime network."

"Mmhmm, she probably put a tracker on your car." Joelle raised a finger and made circles near her head. "Sounds cuckoo. Davon doesn't know he got him a Brandi Web trying to holler at him. You better go save your man."

I frowned. "Who is that?"

"That was Lynn Whitfield's character in that movie with Martin Lawrence." She frowned and shook her head. "Dang, you need to get up on your when-flings-go-wrong films."

I smirked. "The movie is *A Thin Line Between Love and Hate*. I remember the movies, but not the character names. Anyway, I don't think she's that intense, but if I were him, I don't think she'd get a chance to meet my parents."

A few customers approached, which gave me a break from Joelle's twenty questions. I knew I didn't owe Laila anything. I also didn't think there was anything to worry about when it came to Davon choosing her over me. She'd been with him for an entire year and he didn't come back claiming her as his woman. But the baby could be a game-changer. What if he decided he'd be with her for the sake of their child? I couldn't blame him if he decided to at least give them a try.

"Okay, so back to our conversation," Joelle started as the last customer left. "I think you should text her and say, all is fair in love and war, and she can go after him all she wants, but you aren't backing down."

"I don't know, Jo. I could pursue him, start dating him, and then Laila tells him about the pregnancy after we've been together for a few months. Then he would find out I knew and it would create a strain. He would see this woman who brought life into the world, and fall in love with her."

Joelle rolled her eyes. "If she's pregnant, this scenario could happen regardless of if she tells him she's pregnant now or later. You can't control any of it. The only thing you can control is your actions and what you decide to do about this."

"I hear you, but it would hurt less to let her have this small window of time to get her affairs in order. This will also give him a chance to think about what he wants to do. I mean, you're a mother… you can relate to her on that part, right?" I shifted my weight and leaned against the desk. "What's two weeks? Those two weeks could help her realize it's not gonna happen and keep her out of my relationship with him. If there's even anything there."

Joelle shook her head. "I can appreciate what you're trying to do. Yes, I am a mother, and I wouldn't want my family separated. But I'm also a realist. If he wanted to be with her, he had an entire year to make a declaration of love and he didn't. I don't think he loves her and I'm betting she's not even pregnant."

"Okay. So, what if we're not compatible? I could blow up his whole life for what? A few flirty moments in the airport? We can't build anything off of that. He and Laila have history. And the universe clearly doesn't want Davon and me to be together. Maybe she's the right one for him and I just need to back off."

Joelle rolled her eyes. "Girl, please. You two have been yielding for so long, but you don't have to be on pause anymore. You've got the green light. Press the gas and get going."

"I hear you. I guess what makes it hard for me is I know how I feel, and I think I know how he feels, but a lot can change in a year." I closed my eyes and touched my lips, which seemed to be my routine every time I recalled my first kiss with Davon. When I opened my eyes, Joelle was gawking at me.

Her eyes widened. "Oh, my gosh. Y'all did kiss? I knew it was more than lunch that day. This is why your nose is wide open. That must have been some kiss."

I bit down on my bottom lip and blushed. "Ugh. It felt so right. When our lips touched, it wasn't awkward at all. In fact, it felt familiar. But hey, who is to say the magic would still be there?"

Joelle nudged me and said, "That's why you need to call him and get some more practice in. Your tongue is probably dry from lack of use."

I snorted out a laugh and thumped Joelle's knuckles. "Shut up! You are too much. I can't take you."

"You don't need to worry about me. You need to be trying to find out more about Davon. Go worry about him. As a matter of fact, hand me your phone. I'm sick of this."

She reached under the counter to grab my phone and I snatched it away. "Look, chill out lady before I call security on you."

"Whatever. So, what are you gonna do?" Joelle crossed her arms and sighed. "And before you say anything about the baby, I need you to see a pregnancy test and get confirmation from Davon that Laila's with child. She might be making that up. You don't know her and you said it yourself, if he wanted her, they would already be together. You can't keep putting your life on hold. You've waited long enough."

"Yeah. You're right. I wonder if she really changed my number in his phone or if he just hasn't called," I mumbled.

"Enough already. I love you but you are annoying. Woman up and call him? Or send him a text? Or hush talking about him and Laila. You deserve to be happy and I think Davon is the one for you." She exhaled. "Tell yourself the truth, you two have always had chemistry. Even before the kiss. All you need to do is tell him you're ready and available, and I bet you he's gonna come running to see about you."

An older gentleman approached the counter with a wide grin on his face. I returned the smile and said, "Hello. How may we help you, sir?"

"I'm sorry. I didn't need anything, you just remind me so much of my granddaughter," he said.

Confused, I laughed out of pure awkwardness. "Oh, do I look like her?"

"Hell, no," he said. "She's old and grouchy. You seem friendly and you're way younger."

I looked at Joelle and we both snickered. I didn't know what he was getting at, but out of respect for my elders, I would listen continue listening to see what he was trying to say.

"Sir, what is it about Audrienne that reminds you of your granddaughter?" Joelle asked.

He leaned in closer. "Well, you like to talk about the problem but aren't willing to work on fixing it."

My brow lifted. "I'm sorry, I don't follow."

"I couldn't help but overhear your conversation." He shrugged. "My niece had a young man falling all over himself for her, and she let him get away. She always said if she saw him again and he was single, she was gonna tell him how much she loved him. But she never got the opportunity because the next time she saw him was at his funeral."

Joelle and I exchanged a glance. I frowned and held my hand close to my heart. "That's an awful story."

He nodded. "The moral of the story is, it takes time to find love but the one you love won't always be here. Make sure they know how much you care while you can still tell them."

As he ambled back to his seat, I turned to Joelle with my lips poked out. "Oh my gosh. My heart can't take it."

Joelle swiped at her eyes and leaned down to grab my

phone. "Take your cell and go call him. You can't tell me you're still going to give up. Call him."

I sighed. After hearing that story, I couldn't imagine not shooting my shot with Davon. I grabbed my phone and sent a quick text and then put my phone away.

"Did you text him?" Joelle asked, her eyes beaming.

I shook my head. "I can't. You must have forgotten that Laila blocked my number in his phone. I would use yours but I want to talk to her first. I want her to know she can do her absolute worst to try to block me from Davon, but I'm not backing off so she might as well get prepared for a battle of the heart. And I'm playing to win."

TEN

Three days passed before Laila said she was free to meet with me, which just so happened to be a Saturday and my only day off. I think it was strategic, and she wanted to make sure she had more time with Davon. It was cool though. Because after today, her game of keep-away was coming to an end. I had let her control the narrative, but today I planned to tell her exactly how I felt about her proposal and be vocal about what I wanted.

I asked Laila to meet me back at the Bobby Blues Diner. This time, I was the first to arrive and she was now ten minutes late. Of course, when I was the one asking to meet up, Laila decided to take her time getting here. I couldn't help but think she was stalling. Either way, I couldn't continue to let things go on as they had. Enough was enough.

I took a napkin from the dispenser on the table and started to twist it in my hands. I wasn't sure why I was so nervous. I knew what I wanted to address and unlike last time, I called this meeting, so why was I so anxious? My head snapped up as the chimes on the door clang, indicating someone was entering and that someone was Laila.

She had gotten her hair pressed out or maybe it was a

sew-in. I wasn't sure but the long strides she took towards the table made her hair move in R&B singer, wind-machine motions. She looked radiant in her winter white sweater and caramel-colored, corduroy pants. The petty in me couldn't help but notice she had her hair parted down the middle. Not that I owned that hairstyle, but I couldn't help but think she decided on this look because Davon had complimented my hair when I wore it that way. I guess she figured she'd make it work for her too.

"Sorry for being late," she said as she slid into the booth. "The traffic was horrible on the way here."

"No worries," I said. "I've lived here all my life and the traffic gets crazier every year as they to build more homes."

The waitress came over to take our order. I asked for a cup of coffee and Laila held up two fingers to indicate she'd take a cup as well.

"So, Laila, I see you switched up the hairstyle. It looks nice."

Her cheeks reddened as her hand went to stroke her tresses. Her reaction made me feel my thoughts were vindicated. "Um, thanks. Yeah. Change can be good."

I smirked. "I couldn't agree more. It's good to try new things or move on from things which are no longer benefiting us."

She nodded. It was clear she caught the slight shade I tossed in there for good measure. "Right. So… I'm guessing we're here so you can tell me your decision. Is that right?"

"Yes, I thought it would be more appropriate for us to talk in person. I've been thinking about it, and I don't feel like it's meant for either of us to decide for Davon. He should hear from both of us, and he can decide what he wants to do."

The waitress returned with two mugs and a pot of freshly brewed coffee. The steam touched my face and the aroma kissed the tip of my nose. I smiled as she poured. Laila, on the other hand, rested her elbows on the table and rested her chin on top of her hands. She stared at me the entire time. I guess she could care less about the coffee.

She thanked the waitress and said to me, "Is this your way of confessing? Did you call and tell him everything before I arrived?"

"I haven't told him anything yet. You blocked my number in his phone. Remember?" I licked my teeth and chuckled. There was nothing to laugh about. This was one of those laughs reserved for calling on Jesus when I needed him to keep me from acting a fool. "Oh yeah, and I noticed I couldn't find his social media page anymore. Guess you blocked that too?

Laila's lips twisted as she fought back a smile. "Oops. I forgot to mention that one to you. My bad."

This heifer was trying to be funny. She knew what she'd done. I had to move this conversation along before one of us took a swing at the other.

"Was Davon happy to hear he was going to be a father? And how did he react to you saying you wanted to be his woman?"

Her mouth gaped open and she shook her head. "I haven't spoken to him about that yet. I was waiting to hear from you."

"Wow. Why would you wait to hear from me to tell him he's going to be a father? My telling him I'm single and want to date him, won't change the fact that he's going to be a dad. Unless you're lying? Cause none of this makes sense."

Laila started to shift in her seat. While my eyes were trained on her, she all of a sudden found interest in the salt and pepper shakers on the table. When seconds passed without a response from her, I repeated myself.

"Laila, why haven't you told Davon about the baby or how you feel about him?"

A line etched between her brows as she frowned. "I still don't see why I need to verbalize my feelings when my actions are showing him how I feel. It's not like you had to tell him how you felt about him, and he's smitten with you."

I took a sip of my coffee and hoped the rim of the cup would hide my amusement. I didn't get why she didn't just walk away. If she'd showed him interest and it wasn't being reciprocated, common sense should've told her to move on. It didn't make sense to me. I pushed my cup aside and leaned into the table. "Can I ask you a question?"

She looked heavenward and shrugged as if she knew what I was about to say. "Yeah. What is it?"

"If you've done everything to show Davon you're interested and he's still not pursuing you, why don't you move on?" I shrugged. "I don't get it. If you weren't pregnant, would you be more inclined to walk away?"

Her lower lip trembled as she said, "I think I'm in love with him. And I don't want to be a single mother nor do I want Davon to just be my baby's father. I want us to be a family."

My shoulders slumped. I had speculated that Laila loved Davon but to hear her say it was a reality check. Love is a hard emotion to turn off, which meant she wasn't going to go away without a fight.

"At what point did you know you were in love with him? I don't know you, but I'm willing to bet you fell in love with him the minute he mentioned me. It's not for me to understand, but nothing you're doing makes sense. You spent an entire year with him, but never once did you tell him you loved him. Now when he returns home, you want to declare your love. It's now been a week since you asked me to give you time to talk to him and you haven't told him anything."

She pinched the bridge of her nose and sighed. "You're right. It's not for you to understand. And since you're concerned with my actions, I guess it's my turn to ask why you want a man who you say you hardly know. Isn't that what you said the last time we were at this diner?"

I smirked. "Yes, I did say I was getting to know him, but no one can deny our connection. We've spoken on several occasions and have shared parts of our lives. But more than anything, what keeps me wanting to explore a relationship with him is this magnetic pull that makes it hard for me to stay away. And when we kissed—"

"You kissed him?" Laila interrupted. "When did this happen? He didn't mention anything about you two kissing. You're lying."

I closed my eyes and took a deep breath. I tilted my head and looked at Laila. "Why would I need to lie to you? Or care to tell you something outside of the truth? I'll leave the trickery to you."

"Seriously? You're trying to get in my head. You tried to come across as such a sweetheart, but only a conniving woman would play these types of games and try to separate a man from his family. Ugh. I can't stand thirsty women," she blustered.

I chuckled and shook my head. It was clear my telling Laila about my kissing Davon had her shook. "You sound ridiculous right now. It's not like I slept with him and got pregnant. And anyway, I kissed Davon before I even knew you existed and—you're not even his woman. He likely didn't tell you because it doesn't concern you. And you know what, the only person playing games around here is you. I wouldn't be surprised if you're lying about being pregnant."

Laila's head flew back as she cackled. "Please. You should mind your business. And before you judge me, let us not forget, you may be single now, but you weren't single then. I'm sure you pretended everything was okay with your man and didn't tell him about the kiss. That sounds like a selfish person who is trying to have her cake and eat it too."

"Yes, I did have a boyfriend then, and Davon knew what my situation was. We didn't plan to kiss—the universe just brought our lips together," I said with a laugh. "Either way, it happened and I ended things with my boyfriend shortly after. Anyway, as I was saying, when Davon and I kissed we had a connection and I feel certain he's interested in seeing where things go. Whether you tell Davon your pregnant, interested, or whatever you come up with. I'm going to reach out to him today and let him know how I feel."

Laila's shoulders slouched as she leaned back against the seat. "I've never even kissed him. Maybe he and I would have sparks too."

I relaxed my shoulders. Things had gotten tense but just like that, I felt sorry for her. I recall being in deep like with guys when I was younger but they weren't feeling me. I wondered if this was the case for her. Maybe what she was feeling was infatuation but she was confusing it with love.

"Are you sure you aren't just in love with the idea of Davon?" Laila winced, but I continued because we weren't getting anywhere. "Maybe he was your safety net guy. I could only imagine how it made you feel to hear him talking about me. I'm sure if you were seeing someone, it wouldn't have phased you for him to find someone he's interested in. We aren't getting any younger, and I bet the idea of losing him, for lack of a better word, made you desperate for his attention."

"You trying to Iyanla me?" She said it with a straight face before she burst into laughter. "You've made some strong and valid points. Davon is the type of guy you marry. He's always been that and I missed out. It's a painful reality to be heading into my forties and listening to the one who got away talking about this woman he's into and it's not you."

I inhaled and nodded. We were finally getting somewhere. "I understand. I promise I do. I just turned forty last year and I'm sure this is why I stayed in my relationship as long as I did. It was safe and I invested so much time in a dead-end relationship. I didn't want to walk away only for him to meet someone new months later and marry her. I stayed for all the wrong reasons."

We exchanged silent stares for a few minutes before she smiled. "You know, I like you and if I'm being honest, you and Davon are probably perfect for each other." She rolled her eyes and laughed bitterly. "Listen, I'm going to tell him what I did with his phone so he can pick up his long face. He was so confused because he knew he'd texted you before, but he couldn't figure out why he could no longer get in touch with you. I convinced him you'd blocked him and that's why he couldn't reach you."

"You did what?" I shrieked. "I knew you told me you'd blocked my number but I can't believe you lied on me. Actually, I guess I shouldn't be surprised. And here I am trying to be understanding."

She held up her hands. "I know, I know. I'm awful, but I have a way to make it up to you and Davon. Trust me. You won't be disappointed."

"Okay. I'll let you fix it. But call him right now, because I'm not trusting you to do the right thing once you leave here." She forced a smile but reached into her tote to grab her cell. "And put it on speaker. I want to hear both sides of this conversation and jump in as I see fit."

She frowned and shook her head, but did as she was told. "Fine. I don't think this is necessary but I guess I owe you this much."

I nodded. "You do. And it's not like you need privacy cause I know what you did to me and I know about the baby."

Her face went blank as she scrolled to find his number. "Um, about that... it was the only way to make you—"

I held my hand up and shook my head in disgust. "Just stop. You are certifiable. I knew you weren't pregnant. Wow. After this call, might I suggest counseling? There's nothing wrong with talking to someone about your issues."

She rolled her eyes and hit the call button. I'm glad I told her to call him in front of me. I wasn't sure what her plan was going to be but I wasn't leaving it to fate—especially not with Laila as the conduit. This girl was a trip. I hope for Davon's sake, the project he had with her company was complete. If I were him, I don't think I could be her friend anymore and I wouldn't want to talk to her anymore.

As I listened to the phone ring, my leg started to shake under the table. Once I heard his familiar baritone come through the speaker, I held my breath and waited for the drama to unfold.

Laila looked across the table at me, her eyes filling up with tears as she said, "Hey, Davon. Are you busy? I have something I need to talk to you about something."

ELEVEN

Back at home, I kicked off my shoes, peeled off my clothes, and made my way to the shower. I lathered up my skin and laughed as I thought about my dinner with Laila. She was an odd bird. I wonder if she hid that part of herself from Davon. After the antics she pulled, I would be surprised if she kept her as a friend.

I had wasted so much time trying to play nice. Only to find out this wench lied on me and she wasn't even pregnant. Joelle was gonna have a field day once I told her what a fool I was. I wanted to strangle Laila, but in the end, I came out the real winner. She confessed everything to Davon and he was livid. He promised to call me tonight after he had a chance to digest everything he learned and have a chat with Laila. I don't think she'll be a problem anymore.

I dried off and stepped into my pajamas ready to read a book until I heard from Davon or fell asleep. I picked up my phone to see if there were any messages and smile when I saw I had a text from him.

Davon: Hey Audie. I just finished talking to Laila. Can you talk? I didn't want to call and get you in trouble with your boyfriend.

I looked up from my phone with my mouth hanging wide open. How could I forget? Davon still doesn't know I'm single and the bigger shock is Laila didn't tell him. At least she didn't spoil this moment for me. I couldn't wait to tell Davon.

I pressed the call button on my cell and waited anxiously for him to pick up.

"Audie, hey," Davon said. "I'm glad you called."

"Hey. I'm happy to be able to call," I said, in a hushed tone. Though I called him, hearing his voice still felt like an unexpected yet pleasant surprise.

We sat in silence for a second, and I can't speak for him, but I felt like a high school teenager at this moment. Holding the phone, saying absolutely nothing, and loving every second of it because I was spending this time with my crush. Davon was the first to break the silence.

"My text didn't cause any static did it? I hope not, but after speaking with Laila, I wanted to talk to you and apologize."

I chuckled. "No, you didn't cause any static, but I do want to cling to you. Get it? Like static cling?"

There was a pause and then Davon chuckled. "I see you're trying to steal my crown as the King of Corny jokes."

I smiled into the phone. "Yeah. Or maybe I can stand beside you as the queen."

He sighed. "You know I love the sound of that."

"I'm glad you reached out," I said. "It's been a crazy year and this last month was a doozy all on its own."

He chuckled. "I probably would've reached out to you a long time ago, but Laila—"

"She's a crafty one," I interjected and laughed. "She told me how she edited my number and blocked my number. And told you I had blocked."

"I can't believe she did that. I've known Lai for years and she's never done anything this off the wall. Or well, not that I know about," he said. "I'm sorry for her behavior. I hope this doesn't change how you think of me."

I stretched out on the bed and put the phone on speaker. "It's not like you told her to do those things. She's a grown woman—doing kiddie things."

"I've never seen this side of her. It blew my mind for real," he said. "I guess this is who she always was and I only saw the sweet side."

"Interesting. I was glad she confessed everything, well almost everything. She didn't tell you that she told me she was pregnant. Or that she'd blocked me on your social media page too."

"Oh, heck no. We never even slept together. I've never even kissed her. Wow." I could tell by his tone that he was furious with Laila and this was probably the final straw. "I wish she never would've come to Atlanta. I'm so sorry that I introduced her to you. You don't deserve any of this. Dang. I don't even have words."

"It's not your fault," I said. "I'm guessing you wouldn't have been her friend if you knew she would do something like this."

He released a weighted breath. "I was blindsided. I've never told Laila I was interested in her romantically. I'd never asked her out on dates, tried to kiss her, or anything." He huffed. "Well, the jokes on her now. I blocked her on everything."

"Oh, Lord. Guess I better block her too." We both laughed. I adjusted myself on the pillows and closed my eyes. It felt so good to hear his voice. Even though we were talking about that heifer, Laila. "But hey, I guess you can't blame Laila. You are a good catch and the heart wants what it wants."

"Oh yeah, and what does Audie's heart want?" He sighed. "Don't answer that question. How are things with you and Rodney?

"Over," I said. "I broke up with him last year."

"Audie, you aren't teasing me, are you?" he said. "After my chat with Laila, I'm not sure my heart can take much more."

I chuckled. "No. We got into a big argument, and after talking with you at lunch that day, I had to ask myself what I was holding on to. As you said, five years is a long time to not have an end goal for the relationship—it didn't make sense anymore."

"Excuse me for saying this, but I'm so glad it doesn't make sense anymore." A beat and then, "I can't wait to see you."

"I'm anxious to connect with you too. When I saw you at the airport with Laila, I was a little crushed. I'd been so ready for you to return so I could tell you I was single. I should've sent you a message on your social media page and told you, but I thought it would've been more romantic to tell you in person."

"That would've been nice. Dang. Everything makes so much sense now. Laila rushed me out of the airport quickly that day. She must've suspected you were about to tell me you that would interrupt her plans."

"Yeah, that's what she told me," I said. "But enough about her, I want to see you too. What's your schedule look like?"

He groaned. "I'm headed back to Denver to be with my family for Christmas. I'm flying out Monday. You know Christmas falls on a Wednesday this year. I hoped we could spend a day together. Are you free Sunday night?"

I recalled my conversation with Laila and the part of her plan Davon didn't know about. As she stated, I was not disappointed with her peace offering. I had a surprise for him and needed to think up an excuse to buy me some time until I could tell him the big news.

"Oh, no, I'm not going to be here. I just remembered a few of us were asked to cover the terminal at the Savannah airport. They were short-staffed. Something about a stomach virus. Anyway, I'm flying down there tomorrow morning. I can't believe it slipped my mind. I'm gonna blame it on Laila. I need to get packed. Sorry."

He released a heavy breath. "After all this, we might not get to see each other until after Christmas. Man, Laila is the grinch that stole our Christmas wish, huh?"

I snickered. "Hey, I waited a year for you. I guess I can handle another week. When do you get back? Maybe if I'm not working, I can pick you up from the airport that day."

"I'm only gonna be there a week. I missed a lot not being here for a year, and I can't wait another minute to get to know you. You better be ready for some video chats soon because I'm coming for you."

"I would like that very much," I said. "But you know we don't have to wait, we can video chat now."

"Oh dang. Are you ready to model that satin bonnet for me already? I didn't know you liked me that much. I'm honored."

I snorted. "Whatever. You're too much, Davon. Fine. Guess I'll surprise you with that look later. So, will I talk to you tomorrow?"

"Audie, you won't be able to get rid of me. Don't worry. We're about to make up for the lost time."

I smiled and paused before saying, "While I think what Laila did was wrong, at least the wait let me know for sure just how much I like you, Davon."

"Forget that. She stole a year from me. But I digress, I'm happy to be talking to you now and I don't want us to talk about her again. You get some rest. I'll talk to you soon."

As we disconnected the call, I grinned as I thought about my gift for Davon and how everything was coming into place. My mind had been in a haze thinking about Laila and all of the drama she'd brought into my life, but we found a way to use her knack for plotting schemes to do something good. I still didn't trust her though, so I made a few calls and put a plan B into place. She wasn't about to ruin my plans. I was going to have the best Christmas ever.

TWELVE

Three Days Before Christmas, 2019

Joelle's arms flapped about like she was preparing to take flight as she tore into me about my conversation with Laila. "What do you mean, you didn't slap her upside the head?"

My eyes rounded. I don't know how Joelle's loud, unfiltered commentary still managed to shock me but it did. I shook my head. "Girl, what did I tell you about being all loud? You see last time you had that elderly man all up in my business."

Her head bobbed. "And he gave you some excellent advice, which you took and finally got your man. No, thanks to Laila."

I smiled. "Well, I don't think I'll have to worry about her anymore. She confessed and he saw the type of woman she was. I think that friendship is a thing of the past."

"Better you than me. You have a good heart, Audie. Cause Lord knows I wouldn't have let her off as easy as you did," Joelle said and rolled her eyes.

"It's going to be okay," I said and squeezed her shoulder. "She'll be out of the picture soon. I'm not worried about her."

Joelle's lips twisted. "Nah, what I want to do is call TSA and tell them to hold her up when she arrives for her flight back to Denver. It's nothing to send them a picture of her off social media and boom... detained."

"Joelle, you're a mess." I cut my eyes in Joelle's direction. "Wait, you're kidding, right? Did you set her up for real?"

She looked at me out the corner of her eyes with a Cheshire cat grin on her face. I reeled back and she started to cackle. "Girl, no. I didn't do it, but you say the word, and I'll make it happen."

"You are bad. No, I don't want you to do anything to her. As far as I'm concerned, she's a distant memory and I'm not thinking about her anymore."

Joelle looked at me like I had three heads and a tail. "She told you she changed your number in this man's phone and put lies into his head about you—and it's all good? Maybe, I'm missing something, but please tell me how does one gets away with one offense after the other and you just let it go?"

I stepped up to help a customer, and look over my shoulder at Joelle. "I can show you better than I can tell you, but calm down Jo, I got this under control."

Joelle stepped in to assist the next person in line and asked, "Didn't you say Davon was flying out today?"

"Yeah." I could feel my face warm at the mention of his name. I couldn't wait to see him. To touch his face. Feel his embrace. It'd been a freaking year since we'd kissed and I wanted to taste his lips again. "His flight is in a couple of hours. He should be coming through here soon."

The corners of Joelle's mouth rose. "Look at you beaming over there. Just think, this time next year, you're gonna need a brace to hold up your face from all the smiling you'll be doing."

I winked at her. "I wouldn't be mad about that at all."

Joelle crossed her arms. "Okay, sorry to beat this topic

over the head, but what are you gonna do about Laila inter-fering in the future? I don't see her going away."

I smirked. "I'm not worried about her. She's been handled and I'm pretty sure Davon's done with her."

After Laila told me her plan over dinner that night, I appreciated her effort to correct things and devised a proposal of my own. I bit back a smile as I thought back to that night.

I stepped into the ladies' restroom to make a call. Laila had just told Davon what she'd done and while he gave her an earful, I took a moment to step away. Since she was correcting her mistake, I wanted to make sure she was too distracted to make any future prob-lems for me and Davon.

"Hey Rodney," I said into the phone. "You got a second?"

"Yeah. What's up? Everything a'ight?" he said. "It's been a minute."

"Oh, yes. I'm good. I just need a favor. I have a friend in town and I was gonna tell her about the club. Do you think you can put her on the list and make sure she has a good time?"

"Yeah, I can do that," he said.

"Thanks. And hey, I think she might be your type too."

He chuckled. "Oh yeah? I guess you would know what I like, huh? Well listen, text me her name and tell her to ask for me at the door. I got you."

I disconnected the call and smiled to myself. Rodney was sure to charm Laila, and he might be just what she needed to take care of that pesky, itch she wanted Davon to scratch.

Joelle laughed so hard tears formed in her eyes. "Baaa-bay... you've got to stop. You are killing me. I know good and durn well, you did not hook her up with Rodney?"

I tilted my head to the side and smirked. "That's what I thought would happen, but she ended up hooking up with the owner of the club. Girl, she texted me this morning, apol-ogizing for everything and thanked me for the hook up at the club. Which reminds me, I need to block her number."

"Say, what?" Joelle said. "Well, I guess there's someone for everyone. Either way, it's like you said, she's not your problem anymore."

As we continued to talk about Laila, I looked up in time to see Davon approaching and nudged Joelle.

"Ouch. What was that for?" she whimpered.

Once he was in front of me, he held up his hands and frowned. "What are you doing here? I thought you were flying out to Savannah?"

Joelle looked from me to Davon. "Savannah? What's in Savannah?"

"Yeah. Joelle, a few of us were supposed to cover the Savannah airport. They ended up not needing me." I shrugged. "Sorry I didn't get to tell you, but I figured it would be a nice surprise for me to see you off."

His face softened and he broke into a smile. "Well, when you put it that way, I'm glad things worked out the way they did."

Davon reached across the desk and allowed his fingertips to graze mine. My eyes traveled down to his hand caressing mine and then slowly went back up to meet his gaze. I inhaled. There went that magnetic pull again. I couldn't wait to discover more of this man.

"Hey, Davon. Just gonna ignore me, huh?" Joelle joked.

He turned to her and shook his head. "You know I couldn't forget about you. Let me go ahead and wish you a Merry Christmas."

"Merry, early Christmas to you, too. I heard Santa got you exactly what you wanted on your Christmas list," Joelle joked, tilting her head in my direction.

"Don't mind her. How'd you sleep?" I asked, not moving my hand away from where his hand still lingered.

The corners of his eyes crinkled as he smiled. "I slept well. Someone kept me up all night talking on the phone, but seeing you now has me feeling refreshed."

"Is that right? Well, I can't wait—" I stopped talking as I noticed Joelle listening to our conversation with her hands on her hips and a huge grin on her face. "Joelle, go busy yourself."

She stuck her tongue out at me and turned away to help one of the approaching customers. I stepped around the counter to get closer to Davon. I wanted to feel his arms around me, but I was at work, and besides, there would be plenty of time to be alone with him later.

"You've never been this late for a flight. You always arrive a few hours early before your departure time. Did you get caught up in traffic?"

He nodded. "Atlanta traffic was a beast, and then I couldn't find my boarding pass anywhere. I had to print out a new one. Then Laila was supposed to go back today too. Before everything went down, I'd told her she could catch a ride with me back to the airport. I figured she still needed the ride, but at the last minute, she says she decided to take a later flight. She threw off my schedule." He sighed and stepped forward, taking both of my hands in his. "But I'm here now, and I'm happy to see you. When I get back, I want us to spend some time together. Go ahead and get that on your work calendar. Can you do that?"

"I'm down with some us time." We stared deep into each other's eyes, both fighting the urge to lean in for a kiss. I dropped my head, laughed, and stepped back. "I better get back to work before you won't need me to request time off because I'll just be off—indefinitely."

As Joelle started to announce the zones, Davon looked over his shoulder at me as he disappeared through the doors leading to the gangway. I looked around and smiled when I saw Terri, one of the other gate agents, approaching. She was right on time.

"Hey, Audie. Thanks for the hours. You know I needed this," she said, giving me a quick hug.

"No worries. You're doing me a huge favor," I said. I smoothed out my hair and reached under the desk to grab my purse.

Worry lines etched into Joelle's forehead as she looked back and forth between me and Terri. "Um, what the heck is going on? Did I miss something?"

I turned to her and said, "I'm going to Denver. Laila pushed her flight back. I used my friendly flyer pass and snagged her seat assignment so I could sit next to Davon."

Joelle's eyes grew wide as she yelled, "It's about time. Oh my gosh, I'm so happy for you. But where will you stay?"

"Laila's company has a cabin which they host clients in, and she's booked it for me since they didn't currently have anyone visiting." I winked at Joelle. "It's the least she could do. But don't worry, I have a plan B just in case she tries to screw me over."

I smoothed out my uniform and reached into my bag to hand Joelle my boarding pass. Her hands rested on her cheeks as her mouth hung open.

"Oh my gosh. Well, I don't know what else to say except—I love Laila? Nah, it doesn't feel right. But I love you girl and I'm so happy for you," Joelle exclaimed. She looked me up and down and frowned. "Hold up, I know you ain't going to Denver dressed like that. You'll freeze."

"I checked my bags when I got here this morning, and I'm sure they've already been stored and are ready for flight. I had this all planned out. Don't worry, I'll change once I get there. Now, are you gonna scan my ticket so I can go meet my man?"

She shook out of her haze and scanned my boarding pass. Her eyes started to well up as she passed it back to me. "Audie, you deserve this trip and a chance at real love with someone who sees you and can appreciate all you bring to the table. Enjoy your trip."

I pressed my lips together, fighting back tears of my own

as I hurried down the walkway to board the plane. Once inside the vessel, I looked down at my pass to find my seat number. As I walked down the aisle, I spotted Davon sitting in the window seat with his earbuds in and his eyes closed. I slid into the seat next to him and touched his arm. His eyes fluttered open in alarm before recognition set in and an easy smile spread across his face.

"Hey," he looked from me to the other passengers boarding. "Is everything okay? Did I forget something?"

I smiled as I bit down on my lip. "Actually, yes, I have a Christmas gift for you."

He gave me a quizzical look as he noticed I wasn't carrying anything but my purse. "What is it?"

"Actually, it's a gift for both of us. I always said I wanted a real white Christmas and you said you wanted to be the one to share that moment with me." I reached into my bag and pulled out my boarding pass. "Merry Christmas."

He took the ticket from my hand and his mouth dropped. "Are you serious? Audie, this is the best gift—wait, how did you end up in Laila's seat?"

"She pushed back her flight and I took her seat. It was the least she could do after all of the trouble she caused."

He shook his head in disbelief. "Wow, I can't believe we are finally gonna do this. Now I just need to find us a spot with a fireplace. Since I'm just going to visit family, I didn't reserve a room this time around. I was just planning to stay with my parents."

"I got that covered too," I smiled and clapped my hands. "Laila owed me big time, so I'll be staying at her company's cabin. Or, worst-case scenario, I reserved a room at a hotel. The company cabin has an outdoor jacuzzi tub and a fireplace though, so hopefully, that works out. I know you're staying with your parents but I hope you can join me a few days and make good on some cuddling in front of the fireplace."

He sat stunned and then reached for my hands. "Time with you is the best gift anyone could ever give me."

"I feel the same way. Here's to our first snow-covered Christmas together."

He leaned in and I met him halfway. Our lips connected, and our tongues followed as we let them dance freely, fueled by emotion and desire. His hand stroked my hair, while mine caressed the side of his face. He slid his hand down my back and pulled me closer. I wanted this kiss to last forever.

"Ahem. Can you two lovebirds buckle up?" the flight attendant joked. "All this heat is gonna cause turbulence before we can even make it off the ground. And y'all stay out of my restroom. Y'all look like your version of the mile-high club will take the entire flight. Ain't nobody got time for that."

I dropped my head into his shoulder and laughed. Yes, being in his arms, feeling his lips against mine – this is what I had been missing. We had a long way to go in building a relationship that would last, but I felt like we had something special. I believe in my heart that he's the one who will show me the real love I had been missing. And when love does hit —I hope it feels like Christmas.

Thank you for reading *When Love Hits Like Christmas.*

If you enjoyed reading Audrienne and Davon's story, please be sure to leave a review.

Thank you again for your support.

Continue reading for an excerpt of
Could've Been (A Distant Lover's Novelette)

&

Bells Will Be Ringin' (A Hilson Family
Christmas Novella)

EXCLUSIVE EXCERPT

Could've Been by Michelle Michell

6 months before graduation...

Brandon Carter looked over in Corian's direction. When they were only eighteen years old, he knew she was going to be his wife. He'd feared they wouldn't make it after high school with Corian attending Savannah College of Art and Design's Atlanta campus, and him attending the University of South Carolina, but they managed to make it work. He would drive down to Atlanta on the weekend to spend some time with her and when the weather would allow, they would plan a quick weekend getaway and go to one of her favorite spots in South Georgia—Tybee Island.

Here they were once again, walking along the beach, allowing their toes to sink into the sand as they talked about everything from graduation to plans for the future. With them both graduating in a few months, he wanted to make sure she knew how special she was to him. His four years at USC were filled with thoughts of her and what it would mean to have her as his wife. He'd always been in the background as her friend and confidant, and then one day, they decided to stop running from the inevitable and started dating. Now, he was ready to take it one step further and he hoped she wouldn't refuse him.

"I love coming back here. I have so many memories," Corian reminisced. Savannah was her home before her family moved to Macon when she was eleven years old. "We would go hang out on River Street, visit the candy store, and then we'd come picnic at the beach—we'd stay until the sunset."

"Sounds nice. My parents were always working, so we didn't get the chance to do too much travel," Brandon said. "The most adventure I had was when my folks dropped my cousin and me off at Six Flags."

Corian nodded as she stopped walking to stare out across the ocean. Brandon took this as his cue to put the oversized towel he got from his hotel room, down on the sand to create a space for them to sit. She lowered herself without taking her eyes away from the water. Corian was mesmerized by the ocean, while he stood spellbound by her. He adored her coffee complexion and almond-shaped eyes. Her thick, raven black, shoulder-length hair whipped in the wind and his breath caught. If it were possible, he thought she'd gotten even more beautiful than the last time he saw her.

The sky was lined with streaks of purple, coral, and blush as the sun began to set. Brandon positioned himself behind Corian, he inhaled deeply as a warm sensation coursed through his body from their nearness. As she laid her head back against his chest, closed her eyes, and smiled, he knew she felt it too. With his arms draped across her shoulders, she leaned back and allowed her head to lay against his chest. He rested his chin atop her head, enchanted with the floral scent of her Yves Saint Laurent, Black Opium perfume. His heart rate intensified as he allowed himself to get lost in this intimate, beautiful silence as the serene sounds of the crashing waves washed over them.

She took in a breath and released it as she reached up and stroked the side of his face.

"Hey, babe," she whispered into his locs.

"Hey, pooh." He chuckled. "What's going on up there?"

She giggled and turned her face up towards his. "Just thinking is all. We're about to graduate soon. Life is about to change, you know?"

Brandon lowered his mouth to her ear. "I know what's not changing—me and you. We got plans."

"Oh yeah?" Corian said, the corner of her mouth raising as she turned around to face him. She wrapped her legs around his hips, straddling him so they could be face-to-face as they spoke. "What're your plans?"

Brandon licked his lips and then smiled before saying, "Find you and get married."

Corian rolled her eyes and shook her head as a sly grin formed across her face. "Whatever, B. Stop playing. I've heard this story before."

Brandon tilted his head. "Coco, I was serious then and I'm serious now."

He knew why she was blowing off his desires. When they were in kindergarten, he said she was his wife, but then he ended up playing house with Grace Byers in the play kitchen. When they were in middle school, Corian asked him to the school dance, but he ended up spending his time with Lakeisha Newborn. When he'd asked her to homecoming and then prom, he'd finally made good on his word. Once they were in college, he tried his best to make her a priority as best he could with being in another state, but she still felt his attention was temporary.

"As I was saying," she started, disregarding him, "didn't you mention another internship?"

Brandon sighed. "Corian, stop changing the subject. You're my best friend and the woman I love. You're in my plans, most definitely. You believe me, right?"

Corian shrugged. She scooted back and pulled her knees against her chest. Her eyes bore into him and he could tell she was trying to read him. He knew he made it all sound so simple. To him, it was easy to love her, and he didn't see why planning a life with her should be complicated.

"Listen B, I love you too and you're right, we've always had a special bond, but you're talking about marriage. That's supposed to be forever." She threw her hands up in exasperation. "It can't just be a casual chat like... like, picking a restaurant."

"Since when is choosing a restaurant a quick chat for you?" he said trying to lighten the mood.

Their eyes locked, but no words came to change the awkward direction the conversation was headed in. The only sound was the rolling waves and chatter from the passersby. Corian looked down at her hands and could only assume she was trying to figure out what to say next. He turned his eyes away from her as the jingle of his phone interrupted their private thoughts.

He retrieved his cell from his back pocket and opened it to check his alerts. Corian stood and turned her attention back to the waves in front of her as she considered his words. She did love him and there was no reason to prolong the inevitable—they were meant to be together. Of course, she would marry him. She was smiling so hard she knew she must have looked like a crazed woman. She bit down on her bottom lip. Her love for him rushed through her with such force that her whole body began to quake with anticipation as she waited to tell him how she felt.

"Yoooo. That's what's up," Brandon yelled, startling Corian. She spun in his direction and looked down at him.

"Good grief, B. You trying to scare me to death? What's your problem?"

Brandon jumped to his feet. His long locs fell behind his shoulder as he swept her up in his strong arms.

"B! Put me down," she yelled and laughed, mid-spin. She swatted at him playfully as he placed her on the ground. "What's going on, crazy?"

"That was my advisor. He got a call from his contact at GameTech. They're offering me a job after I graduate. Benefits, temporary housing, and the whole bit. Can you believe it?"

Corian punched a fist into the air before covering her mouth in shock. "That's what's up! I'm so happy for you, baby."

He clapped his hands and paced in front of her. "Yessir. That's what I'm talking about. Woo."

Corian chuckled. She walked over and pushed his dreads away from his face as she got on her tiptoes to kiss him. He pulled her into him and deepened the kiss, running his hands along her spine and up through her tresses.

"Your mom will be relieved to hear this news. Her problem child is making moves."

His smile turned serious as he looked into her eyes. "She would be even happier if I told her my favorite girl was going to be by my side."

Corian looked up toward the sky and bit back a laugh. "Okay, B. You got me, baby. And I got you. We're gonna do this." She chuckled. "I already accepted the job offer at the art gallery in Savannah, but we can make this work. We can rotate our visits, you know? I can drive up to see you and then you can—"

"Coco, listen—" Brandon interjected.

"Or do you think you could work from Savannah? Do they have offices here? Not that Atlanta isn't close—"

"Japan!" he blurted, cutting Corian off. "The job is in Japan."

Corian's eyes widened. She took a step back and frowned. "What? You got me over here ready to jump off a cliff and you didn't think it was important to say how wide the leap was."

He pulled her closer. "Listen, you want to be with me and I want to be with you. Maybe you can start in Savannah and then see if you can find an art gallery in Japan. Please consider coming with me." He licked his lips and stared at her with desperate eyes. "We can be the real-life Whitley and Dwayne. Come with me."

She backed away from his grasp. "Brandon, this is a lot to think about. This is not a decision I can make on the fly. Plus, I'm excited about working at the gallery. I would want to put in some time there, which would mean you would have to wait on me or wait and see if I'm willing to give up the opportunity. Are you willing to wait? You're asking a lot of me."

"Listen, we still got six months for you to consider. For now, let's just table it and enjoy the rest of our summer. Okay?"

He extended his hand and she accepted it, allowing her small hands to disappear in his. Brandon kissed the inside of her wrist, as they started to walk along the beach in silence. He knew Corian, and he was willing to bet her mind was racing with a list of reasons why this long-distance relationship wouldn't work. He, however, was determined to find ways to ensure their relationship endured the hard times ahead.

"Corian, I know you and how your brain works, but there's nothing to worry about." She nodded but didn't say anything. "Our destiny's been written since we were kids. We're supposed to be together."

"Yes, we've always been together and as adults, we made it official," she said. "Heck, we proved long distance wasn't an issue for us, but this is different. Japan is more than a distance—it feels like a lifetime away, Brandon."

He stopped walking and stood in front of her. "Coco, I'm

not trying to blow up your life. You can do Savannah and I'll send for you. I just have to stay hopeful for the day when one of those trips will be a one-way flight. We can make this work. Okay?"

She looked him in the eyes, and he could tell she was searching for what to say. But she never responded to him. Instead, she tilted her head up to engage him in a kiss. He didn't deny her, lowering his lips down to hers. She closed her eyes and he inhaled her scent, both wanting to linger in the moment forever because he knew with each day she would be closer to telling him the truth—it was over.

EXCLUSIVE EXCERPT

Bells Will Be Ringin' by Michelle Michell

I sprinted through the Dallas Fort Worth International Airport determined to make my flight. I woke up late. The story of my pillow-clutching life. I regretted my attire. I wore heels that pinched my feet, black compression leggings meant for the gym, and then there was the poorly buttoned, black and yellow flannel top that clung to me as I hurried through the mass of holiday travelers. I'm pretty sure I clipped a few people with my duffle bag and rolled over a few toes. I spewed a few aimless apologies and kept it moving to my gate.

I should've been in my seat already, but the spat I had on the phone with Charles, my boyfriend of five years, had put a dent in that plan. He drove me crazy—in more ways than one. I loved him, and only wanted to be with him, but he wasn't great at balancing his time. Like right now, he should've been preparing to pick me up from the Hartsfield-Jackson Atlanta International airport upon my arrival, but no – it was more important for him to be with the partners at a cabin in Colorado.

Don't get me wrong. I was supportive of my man and would've loved for him to be the first black partner at his law firm, but I was also a big advocate for all things us. Every year, every Christmas, consisted of him schmoozing clients to impress the partners and not spending time with me. The holidays were major in my family, and neither one of us wanted to force the other to choose. But this Christmas, I wanted him to be there to support me as I walked into what might be a hornet's nest of drama with my siblings. I shook away my thoughts and returned my focus to the holiday hustle and bustle of the airport.

The announcement of reminders about not leaving unattended bags and changes in departure made my heart race at the same speed as my feet as I hurdled over bags and did spin moves that could've gotten me drafted by any NBA or NFL team. Determined not to miss my flight, I picked up my pace. My ankles burned and my calves were going to be killer after this workout, but it was worth it once I got to my destination.

I managed to get to the gate right as they were boarding the last zone. Considering I would be the last to board, I was glad I decided to check the majority of my luggage. I was sure the overhead bins were near full by now, but I was going to make my duffle bag fit one way or the other.

Running my fingers through my short, coily hair, I hustled down the narrow aisle to get to my seat. I'd spent a little extra to get some leg room. Being tall and traveling in cramped spaces, I had learned it was well worth the investment.

I looked down at my seatmate, who had his earbuds in and hadn't noticed I was looming in the aisle waiting to sit down.

"Excuse me. Would you mind letting me in?"

"Oh, I'm sorry. Here, let me get up so you can get by."

He smiled as he rose, and I noticed a slight snaggletooth. Taking in his burly frame, I assumed he played football at some point in his life. Average looking guy.

"Thank you," I said, as I settled into my seat.

Out the corner of my eye, I continued to study him. Probably much longer than what was socially acceptable, but I had watched one too many ID channel marathons to drop my guard. As he turned his head in my direction, I gave a fake smile and waited for the airplane banter to commence. My flight routine consisted of boarding, reading, and sleeping. I hoped this chat would prove him to not be crazy so I could relax.

"So you going to Atlanta to visit or that's home?"

"Home," I replied. "I was here for a three-day National Association of Realtors Conference and Expo."

Real estate was a career I stumbled into after attending an open house with my friend Keesa Swain, who spent years working in real estate before getting her license to be a broker. I had always had an interest in interior design and helped Keesa stage the houses she sold. Once Keesa told me she wanted to start her own real estate agency, I took the steps toward getting my real estate license. That was two years ago, and we'd been working together ever since. Around Atlanta, we had been christened as Queens of the Hunt, because we found our clients the home of their dreams.

"Oh, ok. Commercial real estate?"

"No, I'm in residential real estate," I replied. "What do you do?"

I had to take his focus off me. Before I told him anything further, I needed to see if he was a contact worth making. I wasn't risking my life for some clown who wasn't in the market for a home and had the potential of stalking me for sport. No thanks. He would not be collecting my skin today.

"I'm a scout for the Atlanta Falcons, and I'm Felix, by the way. I was out here following up on some prospects at the Frisco Bowl."

My eyes widened. "Oh wow...I'm Harper, probably your new best friend. My family is full of die-hard Falcon fans.

With the exception of my mother. She was misguided as a child and cheers for the Saints. It's always interesting in our house when we play them."

Felix guffawed. "I bet. It's like that in my family too, but we're split between the Packers and the Bears."

This time I laughed. "Oh yeah, that's some beef right there." I nodded as I made a mental note to give him my card. "Well, I won't continue to chew your ear off. I'm about to plug in these ear buds and catch up on some reading. Once I get to my mother's house, there'll be no rest and relaxation for me."

He nodded and reclined his seat. Guess he wanted a reprieve, too.

As I flipped through the pages of *Sister Surrogate* by LaChelle Weaver, I thought about my siblings and the tension awaiting me once I got to my parents' house. This time last year, I got way too involved in my sister, Wesleigh, and my brother, Donovan's, lives. I got it honest though, because my mother always said as the big sister, I should work towards helping them grow by leading as a good example.

So when my sister was about to make a huge career decision without doing her research, I stepped in and managed to disrupt what she still to this day believes was the opportunity of a lifetime. Then there was my brother, Donovan, who was so in love with his now ex, Paula. She wasn't right for him, but I couldn't allow him to figure it out on his own.

Now they're both upset with me for getting too involved, and my mother blames me for ruining Christmas since it all blew up right there during our annual Christmas Eve dinner. I get it, but it was my mother who always wanted me to get involved in their lives and overplay the big sister role. It's not my fault I was trained to be the dream killer.

I gave up on my book, reclined my seat and closed my eyes. The more I thought about seeing my family, I realized this might be the most peace I would have for the next few days.

Two hours later, my newfound friend Felix and I were both waiting for our bags in the baggage claim area. I pulled out my phone to request an Uber to take me to my house. Charles drove me to the airport for my trip to Texas, and since he changed our plans, I now needed a way home.

I looked over and saw Felix on his phone. My plan was to get his card and some of his NFL contacts. Football players needed a home and I needed to make a sale.

"Felix, thanks again for everything. Can I get your card? Here's mine. I'd love to help you or some of your new recruits, *ahem*, find a new house," I offered.

He pulled out his wallet and retrieved a card. "Thanks. That would be great. I do have a few recruits I hope to sign here soon, so this works out great."

As he began to walk toward the exit, I extended the handle on my bag and rolled out right behind him. As I looked for my Uber driver, who was supposed to be in a midnight blue, Jeep Grand Cherokee, I saw a beautiful redhead step out of the car to meet Felix. The glacier on her left hand let me know she was his fiancée. I needed to say hello. Maybe they needed a house, too. New wife, new beginnings…it was a no brainer really.

"Welcome home, baby," she greeted. He lifted her off the ground. They kissed. "How was your flight?"

"Good, but not as good as it is to see you. I missed you, girl," Felix said, planting a deep kiss on her lips and gripping her behind.

I looked away. I felt like I was violating their privacy. After they loaded the car, I hustled over to introduce myself.

"Excuse me, hi—I'm so sorry to interrupt. I sat by your fiancé on the flight and I couldn't help but notice this glacier you got on your finger. Congrats."

She squinted her eyes, studying me. I began smoothing out my wrinkled attire self-consciously.

Felix chuckled at the awkward exchange. "Meeghan, meet Harper Hilson. She's in real estate. I told her I might have a few rookies who might be interested in a home. I guess she thinks we might be in the market here soon, too."

Meeghan finally smiled in my direction. I guess the thought of buying a house changed her disposition. She shook off whatever was on her mind and spoke. "Talk about divine intervention. God is so awesome," Meeghan squealed.

I smirked. Looking back and forth between Felix and Meeghan, I asked, "Did I miss something?"

"Oh, I'm sorry," Meeghan said, shaking her head. "I hadn't had a chance to tell Felix yet, but the offer we put on a home fell through. The appraisal came back lower than the seller was willing to go. So we're actually on the market —again."

"How unfortunate. I'm sorry to hear that, but I'd be lying if I didn't say I'd love to help you secure a home."

Meeghan put her arms around Felix's back, leaned in close, and looked up at him. "That's definitely something for us to consider, baby."

"Well, you might hear from us soon, Ms. Hilson," Felix said.

"Hilson?" She snapped her fingers. "You wouldn't happen to be related to Wesleigh Hilson, would you? I'm a member at her gym."

I smiled proudly. "Yes, that's my younger sister."

"Oh, super cool. Maybe I'll see you for one of her legendary spin classes in the near future."

I chuckled. "That's highly unlikely. I'm one and done."

They waved their goodbyes and turned to get into the car. As they drove away, my Uber driver pulled up.

"Hello. Sorry about that. It was crazy trying to get over here to you and you know Atlanta PD doesn't play about being parked out here," the young man, identified as Kwesi on the Uber app, said.

"No problem at all. I'm glad you were close by and my wait was minimal," I stated.

Sliding into the car, I leaned my head back on the seat and relaxed. I hoped I got to my mom's house before at least one of my siblings. The last one to arrive was always burdened with the undesirable Christmas tasks like untangling lights and sorting through tinsel and ornaments from Christmas past. The thought made me smile. In reality, I didn't care what I got assigned. I was just happy to be with my family for another holiday.

Try as I might to focus on the happier memories, I couldn't shake the nagging feeling that this would be a not so merry Christmas. After what I had done to my siblings, I had no clue what was waiting for me once I walked through the door. I squirmed in my seat, no longer feeling optimistic about returning home for the holidays. But no matter what happened, I resolved to keep my nose out of others people's business—at least for the rest of this year. No, period.

Yes sir, Harper Hilson's days of being nosey were over. From here on out, I would mind my business and only offer help if asked. Feeling confident about my decision, I sunk further into the seat and looked out the window. This year would be different. I could feel it.

ABOUT THE AUTHOR

Michelle Mitchell, Georgia native, is the author of *Truth Is...*, *INFAMOUS, Bells Will Be Ringin': A Hilson Family Christmas novella, Could've Been, and Kissing Strangers: Tainted Love*.

She has always had a passion for writing from poetry to song lyrics, and her new love, writing fiction. What she loves most about writing is that it offers the opportunity to take readers on a mental getaway using the artistry of the written word. Michelle is currently working on the next installment in the Hilson family and Kissing Strangers series.

When she's not writing, she enjoys reading, trying new restaurants, singing, and watching the Atlanta Falcons. She loves to laugh and comes from a large family full of jokers. Michelle is married and shares a dog baby with her husband, Albert. She's an alumna of Georgia Southern University and still resides in Georgia. You can write to her at authormichellemitchell@gmail.com or visit her at www.authormichellemitchell.com.

Stay Connected
Facebook: www.facebook.com/AuthorMichelleMitchell
Twitter: https://twitter.com/expbutterflies
Goodreads: https://www.goodreads.com/author/show/15009663.Michelle_Mitchell
Instagram: www.instagram.com/authormichellemitchell